He plans to keep me here. Something snaps in my mind, and I go at the door like I'm crazed, slamming into it with my body, not caring about the way it jars my teeth, my bones, hurts my shoulder. I batter the door, clawing and kicking and screaming until I'm sobbing with exhaustion.

I sink to the floor, trembling and feeling sick. I hurt all over, I have to pee, and I am intensely thirsty.

Don't let me die here. Please. I never got to say Never got to tell Mom I'm sorry, tell Dad how luc have him for a father. A whimper wrenches its way throat . . .

STAINED

Cheryl Rainfield

Houghton Mifflin Harcourt
Boston   New York

www.hmhco.com

Text set in Minion Pro

The Library of Congress has cataloged the hardcover edition as follows:
Rainfield, C. A. (Cheryl A.)
Stained / Cheryl Rainfield.
p. cm.
Summary: A teenaged girl bullied for her port-wine stain must summon her personal
strength to survive abduction and horrific abuse at the hands of a deranged killer.
[1. Sexual abuse—Fiction. 2. Kidnapping—Fiction. 3. Survival—Fiction. 4. Body
image—Fiction. 5. Beauty, Personal—Fiction. 6. Birthmarks—Fiction.
7. Psychopaths—Fiction.] I. Title.
PZ7.R1315St 2013
[Fic]—dc23
2012047540

ISBN: 978-0-547-94208-7 hardcover
ISBN: 978-0-544-43947-4 paperback

Manufactured in the United States of America
DOC 10 9 8 7 6 5 4 3 2 1
4500527706

For Jean. You are my family — the loving family I never had.

I feel so loved by you always, and I love you deeply.

You (and Petal) are home.

For everyone who's ever been abused, trapped, or oppressed —

I hope you've found your own way home. Home where you are loved and safe,

home that you've found, created, or been given.

And for every reader who loves a good story —

I hope you find your way into this one.

SARAH
8:00 A.M.

TODAY IS THE DAY I've been waiting for my entire life—the beginning of normal.

I reach for the latest *Seventeen* and flip through its glossy pages until I find the perfect face. The girl is pretty, with wide green eyes, hollow cheekbones, and full, pouty lips. But what I notice most is her smooth, unblemished skin. It's perfect. I cut the photo out and stick it above my bed, in the last of the space. Now I can't even see the sunlight yellow of my walls—but the confidence that shines in these faces is even brighter. And today I'm going to get so much closer to that. I don't care how much the treatments hurt; it'll be worth it. It can't hurt as much as the stares and rude comments I get every day.

I know I shouldn't let people's ignorance get to me. Mom's always telling me I'm beautiful; that it's what's inside that counts. But she's not living in the real world. Sure, whether you're kind or good matters. But pretty people automatically get better treatment. Ugly people get ignored . . . if they're lucky. And me, I get stares, taunts, or people going out of their way to pretend they don't see me.

I try to think of it as fuel for my comic scripts. All heroes have to go through personal trauma before they find their true strength — and most of them feel like outsiders even after they do. Like Clark Kent not being able to save his adopted father from a heart attack even though he's Superman, and his never being able to share his entire self with anyone except his parents. Being an outsider, and always having people react to my face until they get used to me, hurts. That's why I created Diamond.

I've always wanted to have meanness bounce off me the way bullets bounce off Superman. So I made Diamond's skin as strong as a diamond; nothing hurts her. I wish I could be that way; even after sixteen years of this, I still get hurt. But soon all the disgusted looks and whispers are going to stop. I'll be just another face in the crowd. No awkward silences when people look at me, no jokes or clumsy attempts at politeness. Just a regular teen who can fade into her surroundings if she wants to. I tuck the magazine into my backpack.

Excitement flutters in my chest, light and frantic as moths. I wonder if I'll be able to see the difference tonight. If other people will.

I touch my fingers against the smooth skin of my cheek. I

can't feel where the purple begins and ends, aside from it being slightly warmer, but I know exactly where it is — it spreads out from the right side of my nose, almost to my ear, and comes down to my bottom lip in a lopsided triangle.

I know I'm lucky; it could be worse. The port-wine stain just misses my forehead and eye, which means I don't have glaucoma, seizures, and brain abnormalities. But I still feel like I'm from another planet. Maybe that's why I love comics so much. Superheroes are always outsiders, and most had difficult childhoods. They feel like *my* people.

I finger comb my hair over the right side of my face. I know from long practice by the weight of my hair and the angle it falls, that it's covering my cheek enough to help me pass. I don't need a mirror to know. Not that I own one.

I grab my backpack. I'm too nervous to eat, and I used up breakfast time anyway, poring over *Seventeen*. I touch the Superman flying across my laptop screen, his face fierce and determined. "Wish me luck," I whisper.

I rush down the stairs, almost tripping on the treads. "I'm ready!" I sing out. This is better than Christmas morning. Better than any birthday I've ever had. I'm finally going to be like everyone else.

I rock to a stop on the bottom step. Dad is standing in the hallway, his face as pale as bone, his cell trembling in his hand.

"Daddy?" I whisper.

Mom is holding him from the side, one hand flat over his heart, the other gripping his back like she can keep him from breaking apart. She's whispering to him earnestly, her face pressed up against his neck. "It'll be okay, Thomas." Her starched shirt's already wrinkled, and her mascara is running.

This is bad. Really bad.

"What is it?" I edge down the last step and swallow the lump of fear in my throat. "Daddy, what's wrong?"

Dad doesn't hear me. His eyes are wide, almost blank, staring like he can't really see me. Mom turns her head — "Sarah, honey" — and stretches out her arm. She pulls me into a three-person hug, and I breathe in her orange-blossom scent, Dad's spicy after-shave, his body odor, and, above all that, the metallic scent of fear.

Mom kisses the top of my head. "It's okay. It's going to be okay." But her voice is high and strained, and Dad is trembling, shivers coming from deep inside him.

"Dad?" I press my cheek against his damp shirt.

Dad blinks. "Sarah." He tries to smile, but it looks more like a grimace. "Honey." His voice is rough with emotion. "We've got to cancel your appointment."

"What?" I stare at him, unable to process his words. "We'll rebook, right?"

"I'm afraid that's out of the question," Mom says primly.

I turn on her. "You *promised* me! You know how much I need this!" I jerk away from them both, Mom's fingers tugging at my shirt.

The floor feels like it's moving beneath me. No treatments and my face will get worse. The best time for treatments is now, when I'm young. I really should have had them as a baby. They know that. They've read all the pamphlets and articles I printed out for them. My discolored skin is only going to get darker, thicker, even lumpy — and attract even more hurtful attention: the stares, the jokes, the laughter. All the things that make me feel like an outsider.

"Sarah, sweetie," Mom says, reaching for me again.

I step back, glaring at her. "You did this!" I scream. "You never wanted me to get the treatments! You're always trying to cram that inner-beauty crap down my throat. But guess what, Mom? People don't care who I am inside; they can't get past my face! I don't know how you can pretend it doesn't matter, when you never had to live like that! You can get anything you want because you're beautiful!"

Mom gasps.

I clap my hand over my mouth. "I'm sorry, I —"

"You listen to me, young lady — not everyone is as shallow as you!" Mom yells, shaking her finger at me. "Looks aren't enough

in this world. And if you haven't figured that out by now—"
She lets her arm drop back by her side, her shoulders slumping.
"Then I don't know what to do with you."

"Hey," Dad says, shaking his head like he's trying to dislodge
water from his ears. "That's enough, both of you." He looks at
me, his gaze coming back into focus. "Sarah, I know you're
disappointed, but you can't talk to your mom that way. Now
apologize."

"I'm sorry," I mutter, my voice sullen even to my ears.

Mom sighs heavily, always the silent guilter. "I'm sorry, too."

"And your mother is not the reason we have to cancel your
appointment," Dad says, his eyes sad. "Something's happened.
At work."

I try to understand what he's saying. Dad is a graphic designer
with his own company. He mostly works with organizations
that make a positive difference, and he does pro bono work for
nonprofits. He says it's his way of putting good into the world.
Sometimes he comes home shaken up by the things he's heard,
like his work right now for a rape crisis center. But he's never
looked like this—as if someone has reached inside and ripped
out his lungs.

I swallow the thick saliva in my throat. I'm being selfish. But
I've hoped so desperately and so long for a chance at normal.

I tighten my lips and try to stop them from trembling. "What happened?" I ask, not wanting to know, yet needing to. "Did another girl—?"

"Nothing like that!" Dad says quickly. "My company — we've been financially gutted."

I stare at him, trying to fit the pieces together.

"Someone embezzled from us," Dad says wearily. "Someone on the inside. I just got the call. We lost more than one hundred thousand that we were given on loan. That we owe the bank."

"Dad!" Fear shudders beneath my rib cage. "That's crazy! I'm so sorry." The words are too little, almost meaningless for something this big. "Are we going to lose the house?"

Dad runs his fingers through his hair, making it stand up. "I don't know. I just don't know."

I struggle to breathe. We've lived here since I was born. I feel like I'm sinking beneath the weight of it all.

But then I look at Dad's drawn face, the muscles pulling at his cheekbones, the dark fear in his eyes. He looks worse than I feel. "Daddy, you can use my college fund to help pay back the bank," I say. "You can have it all."

Dad makes a choking sound like a half laugh, half sob. "No, honey — that's yours. You need it for college, especially now. I only hope the bank doesn't seize it."

I bite my lip. Dad's face is gray and sweating. I wish my college fund could solve this for him, but he's right — it wouldn't make a dent in this big a debt. I almost can't comprehend one hundred thousand dollars. The enormity of it makes me feel like I can't breathe, and it must be so much worse for him. I know he feels responsible for the people who work for him, as well as for Mom and me.

I reach for Dad's hand.

There's a knock on the front door, and the door swings open, bringing a rush of cold, crisp March air, the scent of snow, noisy street sounds full of life. Brian walks in, stamping his feet noisily on the mat, smiling broadly, his skin flushed from the cold. Even coming in from the snow, his suit pants look perfectly creased and clean. I flip my hair over my cheek even more, hiding behind it like a curtain. Brian's one of the Beautiful People — and beautiful people are just as uncomfortable around me as I am around them.

Brian's smile drops. Standing so close to Dad, looking like a model with his dark curly hair, bright blue eyes, and sturdy, dimpled chin, he makes Dad look even worse. Frailer, somehow.

"Hey, should I come back later?" Brian asks, shifting his laptop from one hand to the other.

"No," Dad says abruptly. "You might as well know. Everyone will soon enough. The company's in financial trouble. If you want to look for another job, I understand. I'll give you good references."

Brian rubs his throat. "It can't be that bad, can it?"

"We owe more than a hundred thousand that we don't have. Someone stole it," Dad says abruptly.

"God," Brian says. "Is there anything I can do?" He looks at Mom, then Dad. "Have you phoned the police?"

"First thing," Mom says.

"I'm heading there now," Dad says wearily.

"Well, let me come with you. I'm not going to abandon ship." Brian puts his hand on Dad's sleeve. "Come on; let's see what we can do."

Dad nods slowly and allows himself to be drawn away. He walks unsteadily, like he isn't sure where the floor is.

"I'll take good care of him, Ellen," Brian says over his shoulder. "Don't you worry. He's in good hands."

Brian takes Dad's coat off the hook and helps him into it, as if Dad is sick or very old — and Dad just lets him, like he's forgotten how to dress himself. I'm grateful to Brian, even as I hate that Dad needs him.

Brian looks over at me then, like he can hear my thoughts. His gaze is so intense, it's like we're the only two people in the room. "Hey, Sarah — keep your chin up."

I sigh softly and keep my face angled downward, away from him, hiding behind my hair.

Brian guides Dad out with a last, reassuring smile for Mom. The door shuts behind them, the sound loud in the silence. I want to run after Dad, but instead I stand there, breathing shallowly. The house feels empty, like all the life has drained out of it.

Mom shakes herself. "Well. We still have to get on with our day." She picks a piece of imaginary lint off her suit, then smiles crookedly at me. "I'm sorry about your treatments, hon. I know how much you were depending on them."

"It's okay." I force the words, choking on them.

"Why do you hide your face like that?" Mom pushes my hair back from my cheek, tucking it behind my ear. "You should let people see you."

"Like Mrs. Barton?" I say, shaking my hair back in place.

"That was years ago."

I don't look at her. "I'm going to be late."

Mom sighs again, her cloying orange-blossom scent filling the hall. "You're beautiful, Sarah—inside and out. If some people can't see that, that's their loss."

I've heard her say that so many times, the words are almost meaningless, but I agree so she'll drop it. "Right."

Mom strokes my hair. "You know the treatment is only temporary. The purple would have come back in a few years—and the treatments would have hurt. That's why we didn't want to put you through it."

I bite down hard on my lip. A few years of people smiling at me instead of gawking. A few years of fitting in, of easy conversations, of finally being normal. I would trade almost anything for that. And the discoloration might not come back. She doesn't know for sure. But none of it matters now.

Mom rests her hand on my head. "I wish you could see yourself the way we do —"

"I wish you could understand!"

"Maybe I do," Mom says quietly. "But maybe I want things to get better for you. And I don't think hiding is going to do it."

I grit my teeth to keep from saying something I'll regret.

"Believe it or not, I was shy and withdrawn when I was your age. It wasn't until I broke out of my shell and started making friends that things got better."

"I have friends," I mutter.

"I know you do," Mom says, but she sounds like she's saying the opposite.

I grab my coat. "I've got to go."

SARAH
8:20 A.M.

IT'S SO COLD MY breath puffs out like fog in front of me. Gray
slush sucks at my shoes. I walk fast, not looking at anyone. If I
don't see them staring, they can't hurt me — or that's what I tell
myself. I turn the corner onto a busier street, yank the *Seventeen*
out of my backpack, and toss it into a garbage can.

A beautiful woman's face looks haughtily down at me from a
billboard advertising mascara. I avert my gaze.

Cold wind bites into my cheeks. I automatically rate people
as I pass them, from model beautiful (a ten) to blend-in normal
(a five) to slightly off-putting (a four), but no one ever gets the
rating I give myself — shocking abnormality that is all anyone
can see: what is different, what is wrong (a minus five).

I cut across the street and into the school parking lot, weaving
past the throngs of students gathered in little groups. I tense
against the snickers, the sideways glances, the giggles that embed
themselves into my skin like slivers of metal. It doesn't matter

how many times I tell myself I should be used to it; it still hurts.

I try to slip into Diamond's persona, the way I imagine her — walking tall, confident, and proud — but I can't do it.

The giggling gets louder. I raise my head and steadily look at each kid who's laughing. One by one they turn away. Mom would tell me to stop showing them how much it bothers me and they'll get tired of "teasing" me. But it's been years, and they haven't tired of it yet.

"Sarah! Hey, Sarah!" Madison calls shrilly.

I tense. I shouldn't respond, not after the degrading picture she posted of me online. I can still see that horrible, doctored photo — pus oozing out of the purple stain on my face, flies crawling over my skin. And in big, bold letters: "Why doesn't she just get plastic surgery?" More than thirty students left nasty comments about my cheek, probably because they were scared she'd turn on them next, but knowing that doesn't make it any easier.

Madison calls again, insistently. I know she'll only get louder if I keep ignoring her. I look at her, careful to keep my bad side turned away.

"Got any makeup tips?" she calls. "Like how to hide facial defects? Or maybe your entire face?" The girls around her titter.

I watch her steadily, not flinching, and she turns away.

Madison is pretty — at least a seven. Pretty enough to grab boys' attention. But only a few years ago she had braces, rampant acne, and was twice her current weight. I don't understand how she can act like this — not when she knows what it's like to be laughed at. But maybe that's the point. She doesn't want people to remember the way they used to treat her; she's one of the Beautiful People now.

I walk past her. Gemma nods at me, her short, nubby black hair exposing her scalp to the cold. I nod back but don't stop to talk, even though she seems nice. The resident lesbian and the girl with the purple face would make for great gossip.

"Hey, Sarah," Nick says, edging up beside me.

"Nick," I say resignedly. Nick is almost as much of a social outcast as I am. He has thick glasses; a soft-around-the-edges, plump body; an insatiable interest in comics, computers, and role-playing games, and not enough awareness to not talk about it to anyone who will listen. In other words, a geek. And today he's wearing his puffy silver coat that makes him look like a shiny blimp.

"Thanks for the loan." Nick pulls a graphic novel out of his backpack. *Daniel X.* I lent it to him last week — at the comic shop. I didn't expect him to give it back to me so publicly.

I can just imagine the post Madison will do about this. I reluctantly take the book from him and stuff it in my bag. "Did you like it?"

Nick nods, his glasses bobbing up and down on his nose. "It was amazing."

"I thought you'd enjoy it." There's so much in it we can

both relate to. Feeling alone. Being alone. Wishing we had superpowers to change our world.

Nick pulls another graphic novel out of his bag, and a bunch of markers spill out onto the slush. His face reddens as he bends down to pick them up. "Try this one," he says as he straightens and hands me the novel.

Ghostopolis. I haven't read it yet, but the cover intrigues me.

Behind me, I hear another burst of giggles. I know it's about me and Nick. Purple stain and doughboy. They don't care that he's kind, smart, and good-natured, and sort of cute in a soft, chubby way, with messy, sandy hair that's always falling into his eyes and a quick smile. All they see is his weight and his social awkwardness, just like they only see my face and how alone I am. I glance back at Madison and see her snapping pictures of us with her cell. I yank my hand back. "Maybe later."

Nick blinks, his gentle puppy-dog eyes huge behind his glasses. "Okay," he says fast, and turns away.

I know that move. I've done it so many times myself, trying not to let people see I'm hurt. "Wait!"

Nick turns back to me.

"You show your comics to Mr. Simmons yet?"

"No," Nick says.

"You should! They're way better than anything anyone around here can do. It would give you some cred, you know? Make those bozos see how talented you are."

"I don't need them to see that," Nick says, smiling sadly, like he is so much older than me, or wiser somehow. But he needs to feel accepted just as much as I do.

I know what it's like to care about something so much that you feel like you'll shatter if anyone criticizes it. That's how I feel about my comic-book writing. Nick is the only one who's ever read any of my scripts, and that was by accident. A page fell out of my notebook, and Nick picked it up and read the whole thing before giving it back. I was so scared I hardly heard him tell me how good it was, and how much he liked Diamond. I want to show him more, but I can never quite make myself.

So I guess I should understand. But Nick has more talent than most of the kids at school. Someday he's going to be really well known for his comics, while most of our classmates will work day jobs they hate. "Why not? Maybe they'd leave you alone."

"You know they wouldn't. They'd still tease me just as much," Nick says quietly. "Maybe even more. And if you want me to share my art, you have to share your writing."

I wince.

Nick laughs. "Exactly. Listen — you want to go to the comic store after school, get some hot chocolate on the way?" His eyes are bright with hope. I don't know how he can keep asking when I keep refusing him.

I bite my lip. "I can't; not today. Stuff at home." Which is true. But I always have an excuse.

Nick looks at me, a funny expression on his face. "You're not like them, you know," he says, nodding toward the clumps of students snickering at us. "You're better. Someday you'll realize that."

I stare at him, not knowing what to say.

Nick gives me another sad smile, and I feel like I've let him down somehow. He walks away and doesn't look back.

Charlene's standing by the chainlink fence, waving to me with jerky, exaggerated motions, her breasts and stomach jiggling. I stride over, drop my backpack to the ground, and lean up against the fence beside her, the metal diamonds pressing into my back, even through my coat.

"I thought you weren't coming in until later?" she says.

"Change of plans."

Charlene waits, but I can't talk about it, not right now.

"Well, I've got something for you." She presses a flat, tissue-wrapped rectangle into my hand. "It's for after your treatments."

I tear off the tissue paper. It's a heavy silver rectangle with a Manga girl on the cover saying, "Who's the most beautiful girl in the world? Look inside!" I know, even before I lift the cover, that it is a mirror. I slap the cover back down fast, but not before I get a glimpse of the purple-red stain that distorts my face.

"Thank you," I say, in a too-bright voice like my mom's. "It's perfect."

NICK
8:29 A.M.

I KNOW SARAH DOESN'T *like*-like me, but that doesn't stop me from trying to get her to notice me. To *see* me. Like that will ever happen.

I'm like Clark Kent without the secret hero identity going on. Easily pushed around, easily ignored. But Sarah's my Lois Lane. She's got such guts, facing her tormenters day after day, staring them down, never letting them see they're getting to her.

And she's classy. She doesn't cower from the bullies or rat them out. She just looks at them accusingly, and they turn away. She's so graceful when she does it — and beautiful. God, she's beautiful. Beautiful and smart and kind, when you get to know her, and she loves comics as much as I do. We'd be such an amazing couple on so many levels. She could write the comics; I could do the art. And the rest of the time — well, there would be a lot of kissing involved.

I wish Sarah could see how beautiful she is. And I wish she could see me for who I am. Because I'm right here, loving her. But she never seems to notice.

SARAH
8:30 A.M.

"YOU SURE YOU'RE OKAY?" Charlene asks, frowning. "You look upset."

"I'm fine," I snap.

Charlene looks sideways at me. "Ooo-kay." She pops a stick of gum in her mouth. "Want some?"

I shake my head, though the cinnamon smells good. I don't like to do anything that draws attention to my face when I'm in public if I can help it. And that includes unnecessary chewing.

Charlene stuffs the pack of gum into her backpack, and an empty Cheetos bag and two chocolate-bar wrappers fall out. She pretends not to see them. She must have had a bad night at her dad's.

"*You* okay?" I ask.

"Sure." Charlene chomps on her gum. "My dad only called me a fat cow again last night."

I clench my fists. "What an a-hole!"

Charlene lowers her voice. "He said no boy would ever want me."

"Why do you listen to what he says? Your mom left *him!*"

Charlene shrugs. "He's right. I've never even had a date."

"You'll find someone; don't worry. It just has to be the right someone."

"You mean someone desperate enough or blind enough to date me. If only I could lose a few pounds."

I don't know what to say. I want to tell her she looks just fine to me. I want to tell her she doesn't need a guy. But I don't want to sound like my mom. Besides, she knows the hours I've spent staring at models' faces. How can I tell *her* not to obsess, when I do?

"What does your mom say?"

"That I'll find someone when I'm ready. She's becoming almost as New Age cheerleader as your mom!"

"She sounds more right than your dad, though."

"Whatever." Charlene shrugs, but her face holds pain. "At least she doesn't mention my weight. The weekend can't come soon enough for me."

She blows a bubble, and the sweet cinnamon scent makes my mouth water.

Charlene swallows the bubble so fast she almost chokes. "Get a look at that new guy over there!" She grabs my arm. "Isn't he hot?"

I look. Dark hair, nice cheekbones, and great pecs, wearing

only a black leather jacket over his T-shirt, even in this cold. He grins cockily at the girls flirting with him. He's at least an eight out of ten. What makes him so attractive is the way he slouches in his jeans, an almost dangerous vibe coming off him, like he could really hurt someone if he wanted to. I don't understand the attraction to that type, but it's clear that I am one of the few girls who doesn't.

"It's pretty late in the year to transfer," I say.

"I heard he got kicked out of Central — but that's their loss! He's ours now."

I frown. "That doesn't make him hot. Besides, he's too full of himself. Look at him lapping up the attention."

"I'd lap him up if I could!" Charlene laughs loudly — a laugh meant to grab attention — and, sure enough, Bad Boy turns to look. His gaze lingers on Charlene, on her full belly and wide hips, her large breasts, her round, pretty face — and then he sees me. He stares at my cheek, his lips curling back.

I can feel all the blood rushing to my cheeks. I turn to Charlene, but she's got a goofy smile on her face.

"Come on, Sarah, let's go say hi!" she whispers, digging her fingers into my arm.

I shake her hand off. "No. You go ahead."

"What's with you?"

"Nothing! Just . . . be careful."

Charlene puts her hands on her hips. "You are *so* not okay. Spill!"

A basketball careens toward us, spraying dirty slush. I slap it back. "They canceled my treatments. Told me this morning, just as I was getting ready to leave."

"Oh my god, you're kidding!" Charlene's rosebud mouth parts open. "But you've been planning this for years."

"Something bad happened at my dad's company. He can't afford it right now. I'm so worried about him, Char. It hit him really hard."

"Oh." Charlene's voice is quiet. She knows all about tight budgets and a dad losing his job, struggling to make ends meet. I hope it doesn't hit my dad the way it hit hers. I don't want to see him lose his confidence, turn to drink, get mean. But I can't imagine my dad ever doing that. He has too much integrity.

"What're you going to do?" Charlene asks.

"Get a job, I guess. If I can." But the last time I tried to — the only time I tried — the woman made a big deal of my face. I dig my nails into the palm of my hand. There has to be someplace that will hire me. Some way I can help Dad.

"Hey! I know what you need — a diversion," Charlene says, nudging me. "And the perfect diversion is standing right over there. You're not going to let the Madisons of the world take him, are you?"

"Madison's welcome to him."

Charlene sighs, her hair puffing up off her flushed forehead. "Come on, Sarah. I know you don't like people staring at your face. But this guy actually looked at me. I'm probably the only girl in school who's never been kissed." She blinks as she gazes at me. "Okay, one of the only girls. So do it for me, will you?"

"He doesn't want to talk to me, Char. He wants to talk to you. Now, get yourself over there." I give her a little push.

Charlene licks her lips. "Wish me luck."

I don't want to wish her anything, not with that guy. My cheek is a great jerk-o-meter; it always brings out what is hidden in people. But I force a smile. "Luck."

Charlene gives her body a wiggle, then saunters toward Bad Boy. I want to call out to her, tell her she's worth more, tell her she shouldn't listen to her dad, but I just stand there watching. It didn't used to be like this. We used to sense each other's private despair — Charlene with her plumpness, me with my face — and jolly each other out of it. And that used to be enough. But something's changed.

I feel sad as I watch Charlene laugh with Bad Boy, practically pushing herself onto him. I have never felt so alone.

NICK
11:30 A.M.

I'M WORRIED ABOUT SARAH. She's pale and distracted, not even pretending to listen. I stare at the whiteboard as Mr. Talbot writes out an equation. I wish she would trust me enough to let me in. She looks like she needs someone.

The first time I saw Sarah act all hero-like, she won my heart. It was in fifth grade. She was walking home ahead of me. As I rounded the corner, I saw Sarah running after a group of boys who were taunting Googly Eyes — that's what the other kids called her — a girl with dirty Coke-bottle glasses, her mouth permanently open, and wearing cheap, ill-fitting clothes. I jogged after them, keeping Sarah in sight.

The boys were shoving and laughing at Googly Eyes. Sarah ran right up to them, put herself between them and the girl, her fists up like a boxer, and yelled at them to leave Googly Eyes alone. I thought they might attack her, but when she screamed that they were weak, spineless bullies, those boys took off down the street, running fast. I trailed after Sarah as she put her arm around the girl and walked her the rest of the way home — protecting her like Wonder Woman would. I think that's the day I really fell in love with her.

Sarah became a hero in my eyes that day. But I've never seen her defend herself the way she defends other people. It's like she thinks she doesn't deserve it, or maybe she thinks she doesn't need it. Which is funny. Because what Sarah needs is Sarah. She just doesn't know it yet.

SARAH

I HAVEN'T BEEN ABLE to stop thinking about Dad. I keep seeing his face, how gray it looked, the worry etched deep. I ache from the loss of my dreams, but it's Dad's face that makes me feel like I'm underwater.

I've caught Nick watching me, and I know he knows there's something wrong, but what can I say to him? It's not like we're friends, not the way Charlene and I are. But I almost wish we were. I could use a friend today.

I push out of the heavy school doors into the gray afternoon, cold wind ripping tears from my eyes. The wind snaps my hair back from my cheek. I don't even try to cover it back up; I know it's useless. Behind me, the door crunches open again, then slams shut. Heavy footsteps echo behind me, and I hear male laughter. My skin tightens.

As I turn the corner, I glance back. Bad Boy is trailing me like a shadow. Bad Boy and a group of his new buddies.

I can feel them behind me, their stares burning into my scalp. They are hooting and hollering, trying to make me run. I slow my pace and lift my head higher. Maybe they'll get bored and leave me alone.

People stare at me as they pass — not at the boys following me, acting like hoodlums, but at me, minding my own business.

A little boy looks up at me and points. "Mommy, what's wrong with her face?"

"Shush, honey," the woman says, not meeting my eyes.

My chest tightens. I don't look back at them, though I can feel the woman still watching me.

The boys are closer now, their jeers loud in the street. "What's the hurry, disease girl?"

I speed up, breath jagged in my throat. The dark gray clouds grow heavier and lower.

Out of the corner of my eye, I sense a car keeping pace with me. Another jerk gearing up for an accident, all because he'd rather watch my face than the traffic. I keep my focus on the streetlamp, the mailbox, the dirty store windows that I pass, the children shrieking with laughter as they run through the slush. One of Mom's stock phrases echoes through my head like a litany: *Educate, don't aggravate.* I tell the voice to shut up, but it doesn't go away.

"Hey, burn face!" the new guy shouts. "I'm talking to you."

Cold wind knifes through my coat. I turn around slowly to

show him I'm not scared. There's six of them — five boys . . . and Charlene?

I clench my hands. Charlene is clinging to Bad Boy's arm, a silly smile on her face, her eyes pleading with me to understand. I stare at her, and she looks away.

I take a deep, shuddering breath. "It's not a burn or a disease. It's a port-wine stain." I am my mother's daughter, after all.

"Whatever, freak. Why don't you just get a new face?"

They all laugh, even Charlene. I wish I could gouge the faulty blood vessels out of my flesh and rid myself of this stain.

Charlene giggles again, loud and high pitched, her laughter cutting through the air.

I look at her. "This isn't you," I say quietly. "You're better than this."

One of the guys snickers.

Bad Boy yanks Charlene closer. "You gonna let her talk to you like that?"

Charlene bows her head. "It's no big deal."

"I think it is."

They move faster than I thought they could, enclosing me in a human fence. Pedestrians edge around us in a wide circle, some looking curious, some scared, but not one of them stops. The pawnshop next to us is dark and deserted.

My breath quickens in my chest. Charlene looks uncertain now, her skin pale where there is no makeup.

I shiver and take a step back, almost bumping into the boy behind me. "Look—I didn't do anything to you."

"You showed your ugly face," the new boy says. "You flaunted it."

I *flaunted* it? Did he even see the way I draped my long hair to cover my cheek, bowed my head in class, kept my mouth shut when people laughed at me? I'm the invisible girl, the make-no-waves girl, the pretend-I'm-not-here girl. I hardly take up space. I even breathe more shallowly than other people do.

The sky rumbles ominously, the air around us heavy, growing colder. The new boy reaches into his pocket.

I tighten into myself, getting ready to run.

A horn shrieks in my ears. "Hey!" a man yells. "What do you think you're doing? Leave her alone!"

I can't believe it. No one's ever done that before. I turn to look at my rescuer, at the man who's standing half out of his red car, frowning at us. My eyes widen. It's Brian, Dad's cute assistant. My legs feel weak.

The sky tears open, hail pummeling down like tiny pebbles, bouncing off the cars, the sidewalk, our bodies. Kids squeal and run for cover, women pull their hats down tighter, and men scurry along the sidewalk and rush into doorways. Bad Boy swears and pulls his jacket up over his head. And then he turns and jogs away, the others leaving with him—all except Charlene.

"You okay?" Brian calls, still half out of his car, one hand raised against the hail.

"Yeah — thank you!" I say.

"Want a ride home?" He says it casually, but I feel him waiting for my response. I hesitate. Normally I'd love to spend time with Brian — unsupervised time. But I don't want him to see me like this. "Nah, that's okay."

Brian nods, gets back in his car, and drives off.

I take a deep, quivering breath and let it fill my body. The wind eases up, but now the hail has turned to sleet — cold and wet and biting. Millions of tiny frozen drops sting my skin, coating the cars, the pavement.

Charlene's face is miserable, her hair plastered against her skull. "Sarah, I'm sorry." Her mascara runs down her cheeks in long brown lines.

"Sorry," I say flatly. She stood there laughing at me, not doing anything when they threatened me, and she's *sorry?* It's not enough.

Charlene's shoulders curve inward. "I don't know what came over me. I guess I was flattered by Kirk's attention. I am really, really sorry. Can you forgive me?" Her pain-filled eyes beg me to understand.

I know Charlene feels like an outcast, too. People say mean things about her weight, the way they do about my face. I think of how desperately I wanted my treatments, how nothing else mattered until I saw the pain Dad was in this morning, and I think maybe I understand. "Yeah," I say slowly.

"Friends?" Charlene says.

"Always."

Charlene squeezes my hand, and then she, too, runs off, and I am left standing there on the slick, darkened sidewalk.

SARAH
3:15 P.M.

MY CLOTHES ARE STIFF and heavy with water, and still the sleet
keeps bombarding me, pelting out of the sky like it'll never stop.
People are huddled in doorways, but I don't want to endure the
embarrassed faces, the awkward silences, the glances that slide
away from mine.

I head off down the street, shifting my heavy backpack to
my other shoulder. I can't believe I just had a knight in shining
armor come to my aid. And I can't believe it was Brian.

At the corner I stop for a red sedan that drives up, its
windshield wipers thumping back and forth.

"Hey!" a voice shouts from the car. Brian's voice.

I peer through the sleet at his dark head poking out of the
driver's window. He's getting wet.

"Are you sure you're all right?" Brian yells.

"I'm fine," I call. "Thank you." I turn my bad cheek away from
him. My heart beats faster.

He pulls his car over to the side of the road and gets out, then stands there in the sleet looking at me, his tight brown curls flattening. With his broad shoulders and muscled chest, he looks almost like a superhero in disguise, Bruce Wayne in a suit.

He clears his throat. "You sure you don't want a lift? You're getting soaked. And I don't want to leave you stranded if you think those boys will come back."

My face heats up. I've been staring at him like a lovesick girl. *Get a grip, Sarah.*

I look around. The storm has scattered people, making this corner deserted. "I'm all right," I say. "Really."

"Listen, don't let those idiots get to you, okay? Some people just don't know how to behave. You know — the caveman syndrome."

I laugh. "I call it being a jerk."

"That, too," he says, nodding sagely. He rubs his neck, watching me intently. His curls are plastered to his skull now, yet he still looks handsome. "Your dad told me about your canceled treatments. I'm sorry. That must be rough, on top of everything else."

I shrug, trying to pretend like it's nothing, but I can feel the misery pulling at my face. And I know he can see it, too, because something changes in his eyes. I curse myself. Because, really, losing my treatments is nothing compared to what Dad is going through. "How did it go with the police?" I ask quickly.

"They're looking into it," Brian says. He takes a step closer and rests his hands on his belt buckle. "But they don't have any leads yet. I can fill you in on the drive back to your place."

He stands there, waiting.

"That's okay," I say. "Dad will tell me about it when he gets home."

"He was pretty upset when we left. I'm not sure he heard anything the cops said. But I did. Let me take you home."

Something isn't right. He's pushing too hard to get me to ride with him. I hesitate.

"You know you can trust me." Brian smiles, but there's something almost animal-like in the way his lips curl back, and in the way his eyes watch me, like they're tracking my movements, my reactions.

The hair rises on the back of my neck. I take a step back, then another. "I have to get home." I shouldn't have stood here so long. I turn to run, sleet slicing into my eyes.

Brian's hand closes around my wrist, fingers digging into my skin. Something stings my arm, and then he jerks me back toward him.

"Let me go!" I turn and kick him, but he grips me harder, yanking me forward. My backpack falls into a puddle.

Oh, god. My mind stutters, wanting to shut down. The sky spins around me, and suddenly I am so tired I can barely keep my eyes open. But I have to. I must. I can't let him do this to me. I try to pull my arm out of his grasp, the way they showed us in that self-defense class Mom made me take, but my arms feel like rubber and they won't do what I tell them to.

I've got to get help. I reach into my coat for my cell phone, but my hand doesn't seem connected to my body. I try again, and this time I pull my phone out.

Brian knocks it from my hand. It clatters against the sidewalk, and he kicks it into the gutter.

"Help!" I shout, my voice sounding garbled, but there's no one around to hear.

Brian shoves his cold, wet cheek against mine, his after-shave burning my nostrils. And then something sharp pokes between my shoulder blades. "Don't struggle. I wouldn't want to accidentally cut you open."

The sidewalk moves beneath me. I feel sick. He did something to me. Drugged me. "Let me go!" I kick at him, miss, then kick again. My shoe connects hard. But he is like a machine; nothing seems to hurt him. "Why are you doing this?" I scream. I think I scream; I'm not sure if my voice makes it out of my head. Everything is spinning.

He drags me toward his car. I feel like I'm being pulled through Jell-O, and I just want to sleep. But no, I can't. I wrench my eyes open. The car tilts toward me, the side door like a gaping mouth. I claw at Brian's skin, his clothes, anything I can get my nails into, trying to scream, but my voice won't work.

The world tilts again, my vision blurring, and then darkness sucks me down.

SARAH

I AM COLD AND SHIVERY, my head aching, an oily taste in my mouth. I feel sick, like I might vomit, and I'm more tired than I can ever remember feeling. I don't want to be awake, but there's a reason I have to be. Only I can't remember why.

My skin feels clammy, and my clothes are damp and heavy, weighing me down. Something soft and thick presses against my tongue, my teeth. I can't breathe properly! I try to spit it out, but it won't leave.

The smell of leather and vinyl, wet cloth and pine cologne, makes me feel even more nauseous, like when I used to get carsick on our trips up to the cottage. I just want to lie here and go back to sleep, but something keeps jostling me, making my head vibrate.

Dad, I try to croak. *I had the strangest dream. Nightmare, really.* But I can't make my voice work.

Someone's whistling shrilly, the sound cutting into my

eardrums. I groan and try to push myself upright, but my hands are fastened behind my back, my shoulders sore and aching. My ankles are stuck together, too, my legs cramped in an uncomfortable, bent position. I can't seem to straighten them. I wrench my eyes open.

I'm in the back of a car, stuffed on the floor behind the front seats. I lift my legs. Silver duct tape is wrapped tight around my ankles.

My stomach heaves. *It's true. It's all true.*

I roll on my side and yank at the tape, trying to pull my wrists apart. "Help!" I cry. "Somebody help me!" but the words make only a bleating sound through the cloth.

The whistling stops. "Quiet!"

Why? Can someone hear me? I slam my feet against the door. "Help! Let me out!" I try to shout.

The car swerves. "I said shut up!"

I hammer at the door, every thrust exploding inside my aching head. *Let me out, let me out, let me out!* The car swerves again, pebbles spitting against the windows, and then it lurches to a stop, my face slapping against the front passenger seat.

Tires screech, horns blare, and I pray for an accident, pray for another car to hit us, for anything that will make someone find me.

Brian unfastens his seat belt and whirls around, hoisting himself over the space between the seats. His handsome face is distorted with rage: his eyes are slits, his nostrils flaring, his lips curling back to show his teeth. He looks like a different person than the one I saw this morning, or even than the one who chased the boys away. He looks merciless. Cruel. *How could I not have seen it?*

It seems crazy that his expensive suit is still neatly pressed, his tie perfect, after everything he's done. I push back as far away from him as I can in the cramped space.

"Stop kicking the door," Brian snaps. "This car is still new."

Maybe if I make enough trouble for him, he'll let me go. I slam my feet harder.

There's a click, and then Brian pokes a knife into my side, right through my coat. "I don't have time for this shit. When I tell you to do something, you do it."

I hardly dare to move, to breathe, afraid even the movement of my rib cage will nudge the knife into my flesh.

"Understand?" he says.

Cars are honking like angry geese. *Please, please let someone come up to the car.*

Brian presses the blade harder against me, and my skin burns with pain. His eyes are cold and filled with hate.

A sour taste forms in my mouth beneath the rag. Brian looks like he wants to kill me. *Rape and murder — that's what happens to stupid girls like me, isn't it?* I bite down on the cloth. *No. If he'd wanted to, he would have already. Wouldn't he?*

"Hey — you listening to me? I asked you a question. You going to behave?"

"Yes!" I bleat through the gag, nodding my head exaggeratedly, trying to show how good I'll be.

He grunts and pulls the knife back, tiny feathers floating up into the air, white innards from my down coat. "Good choice." He disappears from my view. The car lurches forward again, my head slamming into the seat behind me, and I gulp-breathe past the gag.

Brian punches the radio on. Jann Arden's haunting voice sings, "Will you remember me when I'm gone?" The words cut into me deeper than Brian's knife, and I stuff back a sob. Brian changes the station to another, and then another, before jabbing it off again. The silence is a relief.

I fight to draw air in through my nose. Brian is so full of vibrating rage that I am sure he would have hurt me, right there on the road, if I pushed him enough. He knows I know who he is. There's no way to pretend I don't. So how can he ever let me go?

I look up through the window at the gray sky and dark, knobby branches we pass. I have to find a way to escape. I can't let him take me wherever he's taking me.

I desperately yank at the tape. The edges dig into my skin.

"What are you doing back there?" Brian asks harshly.

I yank harder. Disjointed images pop into my mind — sad,

shadowy faces of girls who've been raped and murdered. Girls who never made it home. Girls who were on the news.

I twist and contort myself, trying to get free, but the tape won't loosen.

Brian thrusts his arm back, his fingers groping until he finds my arm and squeezes hard. "Lie still or you'll regret it. I swear to god."

Hot tears stream down my face, snot running from my nose, and I have to struggle to breathe. I am all alone with this nice-guy-turned-crazy, and not even my cell to call for help.

I long to feel Dad's strong arms around me, to feel Mom's lips against my forehead, to breathe in Dad's comforting after-shave, but all I can smell is the damp carpet, the sickening smell of Brian's piney cologne, and the overpowering new-car smell.

I want to be home drinking chocolate milk at the kitchen table with Mom, then rushing upstairs to write a new comic. I want to be talking about movies and books with Charlene, listening to music, and laughing about our crazy day. I can't believe I'm here instead, stuffed like a sack of dirt in the back of Brian's car.

I keep seeing Dad's face, knowing his world is collapsing around him. How much worse will this make him feel? And Mom — all that anger and hurt between us, and now I can't even say I'm sorry. I keep hearing myself scream those awful words.

It's not her fault that she's beautiful and I'm . . . the way I am. The tears keep coming, making it harder to breathe. I'll never be able to tell her that I love her.

I wish now I'd gone to every self-defense class Mom wanted to drag me to. Wish I'd never wimped out just because some of the other girls whispered and stared. Maybe if I'd gone to all the classes, I'd have been able to fight Brian off. But it's no use thinking that. I have to find a way to escape now.

I want to beg Brian to let me go, want to tell him that I'm a good person, that I don't deserve any of this, but I know that none of that matters to him. What he's done there's no undoing, no way to make right. If I could spit the gag out, I would beg him anyway. But the gag is dry and uncomfortable in my mouth, and the car keeps speeding forward.

I don't know how long it's been since Brian dragged me into his car, but I know it's been too long. My clothes are already half dry.

I shudder. *Where is he taking me?*

The car turns and slows, and then we're going up and down over bumps, my head smashing into the floor, teeth squeaking against the rag. Brian starts whistling again. I am so cold, I can't stop shivering.

The tires crunch over gravel.

Please let me out of here alive. I swear I'll be a better person!

The car lurches to a stop, and the engine shuts off. Brian stops whistling and just sits there like he's trying to decide whether to hurt me or not.

Don't do it! I scream at him inside my head, scream with all my energy. *Just let me go!* My breathing is harsh against the rag. I'm afraid I'm going to choke.

Fabric creaks against leather. "I'm sorry I scared you, but it was necessary," Brian says gently, as if he's telling me he loves me.

He's not going to let me go.

The car door opens, setting off a mechanical chime and bringing in a gust of cold, bitter air. I hear the wind howling, smell snow, feel the goose bumps rise on my skin, hear a woodpecker drilling away at a tree, then a chickadee cry out. We're not in the city anymore.

Brian's shoes crunch against the gravel and ice. I tighten, waiting, raising my head to watch. He opens the back door, and I slam my feet into his knees.

Brian grunts and grabs my legs. "Shit! Hold still; I'm not going to hurt you."

Yes, you are! I know you are.

He flips me onto my stomach and yanks my head back, and I retch against the stink of his cologne. I buck and heave against him as hard as I can, but I am like a fish flopping in his hands.

Brian straddles me, and I can hardly move. He covers my eyes with a leather blindfold, pulling it tight and jerking my head as he buckles the straps, plunging me into darkness. Then he fastens a strap beneath my chin, the leather nipping into my skin. I can taste fear now in my mouth, in the leather, in my sweat; I can smell the fear pouring off me.

He fumbles with my watch, ripping it from my wrist, then yanks my necklace off too, the chain breaking.

Please don't let me die.

Brian pushes me into the car floor, grit pressing against my cheek. "Hold still, before I gut you by accident."

He moves off me, his heavy hand holding my calf, and saws at the tape around my ankles. Then he is tugging me out, dragging me against the rough mat, my head banging against the floor. I kick and writhe against him, but he hauls me out into the cold and sets me on my feet. I rock unsteadily, my legs cramping and tingling, the bitter wind whipping my face.

Brian pushes me forward into the darkness. "Come on."

I'm not going anywhere with you! I start running blindly, not knowing where I am going, just knowing I'm going away from him, my wrists held awkwardly behind my back, keeping me off balance, feet tripping over the uneven ground, but running still. And then I am falling onto icy gravel, sharp stones piercing my face, my arms, biting through my jeans, drawing blood.

Heavy hands grip my arms. "Did you really think you could get away? You belong to me now."

NICK
5:00 P.M.

SOMETHING'S WRONG WITH SARAH; I'm sure of it. I wish I knew what. She ran off too fast for me to catch up with her, and then Mr. Simmons called me back.

I stare at my cell. In all the time I've had Sarah's number, I've never had the guts to call her. I can't believe that now, when I finally screw up the courage, she isn't picking up.

I speed dial her number again. No answer. I'm starting to get that skin-crawling feeling that something is really wrong. I know I'm being silly. Sarah would never hurt herself, no matter how much pain she's in. But she looked so upset today, like someone had died. I have to know that she's okay.

I grab my bike. I'm going over to her house. Even just a glimpse of her will reassure me. I'll figure out what to say when I get there. The cold wind stings my cheeks as I pedal, the wheels of my bike hissing against the wet asphalt.

Something big was bothering Sarah today—and I wasn't

brave enough to ask her what. But I'm ready to ask her now. I bike faster.

I pace up and down the sidewalk in front of Sarah's house. This is stupid. I came all this way just to chicken out? No. If I want to be worthy of Sarah, I have to be willing to look stupid. Stupider than I usually do.

I stride up the walkway and ring the doorbell.

I hear running footsteps, then Mrs. Meadows yanks open the door. "Sarah?" she says breathlessly. She looks over my shoulder, craning her neck, then fastens her gaze on me. "Are you a friend of Sarah's? Do you know where she is?"

I stare at her. "Isn't she here? I thought —"

"She's not with you?" Her face falls. "She's not with Charlene, either. Sarah hasn't called in, and she's not answering her cell . . ."

A hard, tight pit forms in my stomach. "She hasn't answered my calls, either. Something upset her at school, but . . ."

Mrs. Meadows rubs her hand over her face. "And we gave her bad news this morning. I hope she hasn't . . ." Her voice trails off unsteadily.

I'm suddenly aware of how pale she is. "Do you need to sit down?"

She grips my arm. "When did you last see her?"

"Just after the final bell."

"Something is wrong. It's not like her. She always calls us if she's staying out late. And she wouldn't want to worry her father, not today."

Why not today? I wish I knew what was going on. But Sarah wouldn't run away. Not my Sarah. No, something has happened.

"It's not like her," Mrs. Meadows says again, dread in her voice.

I stand there helplessly, cold seeping into me, right to my bones. I see the fear stretched around Mrs. Meadows's eyes, see it in the way her throat convulsively tightens, and I know I'll remember this moment forever.

Mrs. Meadows bites her lip. "I'm calling the police." She turns away.

"I'll bike down to the comic store and see if she's there," I say. I pray I find her.

SARAH

BRIAN WRENCHES ME UP off the icy gravel, his words echoing in my head: *You belong to me now.*

Numbness spreads through me, dulling my thoughts. I wonder if my mind is trying to protect itself, to keep me from feeling the terror before I die. Or maybe it's whatever drug he shot into me. I need to stay alert.

A whimper escapes me.

No one knows where I am. I clench my stiff hands. I'm not ready to die. I've got so much I still want to do. I want to know what it's like to walk down the street and not have anyone stare at me. I want to get my comic books published. And I want to have a family someday. A family of my own.

My eyes burn.

Let there be someone around to see us. Please, let someone save me.

Brian shoves me forward. "There's a step up," he says. "Three steps."

I hesitate. I don't know where he's taking me, but I know that wherever it is, I shouldn't let him.

His fingers dig into my collarbone. "If you don't move, you won't like what happens next."

I remember his knife in my side. I climb the creaking stairs, each of my steps getting slower and heavier. Maybe I should just run and take my chances. But I can't see which way to go. And how long could I survive in this cold with my hands fastened behind my back?

I stand there, trembling, not knowing what the best thing to do is — the thing that will keep me safe.

Brian pushes me forward.

The air stinks of piss. Not human; animal or rodent. There is a scurrying, scrabbling sound close to my feet. Rodent, then. I stiffen, trying not to react.

Brian presses up behind me, his cologne like a fog clouding my mind. "It's not as crowded as your room is with all those faces staring out at you, but that's part of its charm. Right, Sarah?"

He's seen my bedroom. Maybe even been *in* my bedroom. There's no other way he could know about the faces taped to my walls. It's a private thing, something Dad wouldn't talk about.

I shudder and twist away, but Brian pushes me forward. A door slams shut behind us, echoing hollowly.

Without the wind it's warmer, but not by much.

"Keep still," Brian says, his breath hot against my ear. The gag tightens, pulling at my mouth, and then it jerks back and forth as he saws through the cloth.

My breath quickens. *He's going to let me go!*

But no, that doesn't make sense. I can't let myself think that way.

The sawing stops, and then the cloth is ripped from my sore mouth.

I open and close my dry, aching mouth, run my tongue over my roughened lips. "Let me go," I say hoarsely.

"Don't be absurd." He tightens the strap beneath my chin, and I hear a scape, then a click.

Tears burn at my eyes. *Don't let me die, don't-let-me-die!*

He tugs at the back of the blindfold, jiggling my head. Metal rasps against metal, and my hope fades. I hear another click, like a lock snapping shut, and then he lets me go.

Brian turns me around to face him, drawing me closer. "There. All done," he says, his voice eager and fast, pitched higher than usual.

He's excited. Excited and afraid.

"You could just let me go, and no one would know," I say, my voice trembling.

Brian laughs. "You think I would go to all this trouble and then do that? No, I brought you here to help you."

51

"Help me?" I stifle my anger and fear. *How is this* helping *me?* "I don't need your help."

"Of course you do." He touches my stained cheek with his sweaty fingers.

I jerk away. *Don't touch me!*

"Don't you want to know what it feels like to be normal? To be happy?"

"I *am* happy!"

He trails his fingertips across my cheek. "Are you?"

"I want to go home!" I gulp, choking back the tears.

"Really? But you weren't happy there."

"Yes, I was!"

"Is that why you acted like a spoiled brat when your parents canceled your treatments this morning?"

I suck in my breath. How does he know that? Unless Dad told him. My heart aches. I wish Dad were here with me now.

There's a scrabbling sound again, like mice in the wall.

Brian rubs his face against my cheek. "You don't know it, but you're beautiful."

I want to scream at him to get away from me, but I can't let him see how much he scares me. I wrench away and slam back against a wall, my fingers crushing painfully beneath me.

The floor creaks. He's close to me, still; I can feel it. I try to breathe normally, to not show my fear.

"I'll bet you've waited your whole life just to have someone tell you that," he says.

"My mom's told me a thousand times! I don't need to hear it from you." *From a sicko.*

"You don't really think your mom was telling you the truth? She feels sorry for you, that's all. Just like your father does."

I turn my face away from his voice. I'm not going to let him mess with my mind.

"You know I'm telling you the truth. They feel sorry for you because of this." Brian strokes my purple cheek again.

"You don't know anything!" I slam my knee upward and connect with soft flesh.

He gasps.

I feel cool air against my skin instead of his heat. I run toward where I think the door should be, run with my hands still taped behind my back.

I smash into a wall, my nose crunching, pain bursting through me, hot liquid gushing from my nostrils. Blobs of orange light ooze in front of my eyelids, and I stagger.

"Look what you've done to your pretty face," Brian says from behind me. He grips my chin with his huge hand and turns my head. "That has to hurt. But I'll bet it doesn't hurt as much as people thinking you're a freak."

His voice is raw, too full of pain to be about me. I wish I could see his face to know for sure. I twist my head, trying to get free. "Is that how people treated you? As if you weren't good enough?"

"Don't you try that psychology shit with me. If you can't keep your mouth shut, I'll put the gag back in. Understand?"

"Yes," I croak.

"Good." He pulls his hand away.

My nose hurts like hell. I spit salty blood out of my mouth. I hope I get some on him.

"Stop fighting me, Sarah. I promise I'll let you go — when you're ready."

Why does he keep lying to me? He has to know I don't believe him.

"You and your family have suffered so much. But I'm going to help you."

"We don't need your help."

"Ah, but you do. Every day your parents look at you and wonder if they did the right thing, teaching you to accept yourself when they know the world never will. Sometimes it hurts them so much they can't even look at you."

I take a shaky breath. I am so afraid that what he's saying is true. Deep down, I know it is.

SARAH

ALL THE TIMES SOMEONE was rude to me, and Dad and Mom were with me — I saw my pain mirrored in their faces. And the times when Dad looked away from me, sadness in his eyes. When Mom would give me her "inner beauty" speech after someone hurt me. Maybe it *has* been as hard on my parents as it has been on me. Maybe they even wished they had a different daughter, a pretty one. A normal one, at least.

No. I won't let Brian into my head.

But how do I deal with him? If Mom were here, she'd try to reason with him, make him see that what he's doing is wrong — but I don't think he cares about that. Still, I have to try.

His breathing is loud and fast in my ears. I can't tell anymore if he's excited or afraid. But I know exactly where he is from the sound of his breath and the stench of his cologne. I turn my face toward him. "You can't hold me against my will. Someone will find me. I'll bet my mom's already calling around."

He makes a sound deep in his throat, like a dog growling.

I step back fast, wood creaking beneath me. "She'll be worried if I don't get home soon. And my dad — this will hurt him so much."

"They'll get over it."

"No, they won't; they love me!"

"They feel guilty about you. That's not the same thing."

Tears prick my eyelids. I try to open them, but there is only blackness. "You don't know my parents! Not the way I do."

"I know them better than you do. I've seen it all before." He laughs thinly. "The guilt that churns inside a mother when her child is deformed. The burden that child becomes. The distance, and then the hatred that grows."

I can feel his craziness seeping into my thoughts, can feel myself start to believe him. I've got to keep myself from being sucked into his twisted world. "Please, just let me go."

"I saved you, Sarah. How can you be so ungrateful?"

"You *kidnapped* me!" I edge away from him.

He slams me back against the wall, his sour breath hot on my cheek. A hard lump jabs into the back of my head. "How quickly you forget. Just a few hours ago you were a damsel in distress, and I came to your rescue. Poor little Sarah."

His voice vibrates through me, loud and mocking. I try to analyze every change in his tone, but it's hard to know whether my guesses are right without seeing his face. I know he's looking for something, but I don't know what it is, or what will happen if I give it to him. "The only one I need saving from is you."

Brian chuckles and presses himself against me, his cologne burning my nostrils. "If I'd known you were this entertaining, I would have rescued you sooner. The last girl wasn't half as plucky."

The last girl? I think I'm going to puke. I turn my face away and suck in the fetid air. "They'll come looking for me. People saw you talking to me. They'll find you."

"That's what *you* think. Now, stay still; I'm going to cut you free."

Don't let me die. Please don't let me die.

He gently turns me away from him, then saws at the tape around my wrists, jolting my body with every rhythmic thrust. The tape splits apart, and I ease my aching arms to my sides, my shoulders screeching. My fingers are stiff and cold; just wiggling them sends sharp tingles of pain through my hands.

"I hope you're not in any discomfort," Brian says. "Now, come, I want to show you where you'll be staying."

He drags me forward, then forces my hand down until my fingers touch stiff, new cotton with a soft give, tiny points pricking up through it. Feathers. It must be a down comforter.

"This is where you'll sleep — and where we'll make love."

I rip away. "Don't you touch me!"

"You think you don't want it now, but you will, Sarah. Trust me." He pats my cheek.

I flinch.

"Maybe if you sit here and consider your options, you'll find yourself willing." He laughs. "Make your decision and let me know. I'll be back soon."

Bile rises in my throat.

I hear his footsteps echo on the wood floor, hear the door bang shut, metal grate against metal, the steps shudder. I stand there listening as his car door slams, the motor roars to life, and the tires spit gravel.

I can't believe he's really gone. It has to be a trick.

I listen harder.

The wind howls like a wolf around the edges of my ears. There's no other sound.

This is my chance, the chance I've been waiting for. My chance to get out of here.

NICK
5:45 P.M.

SARAH WASN'T AT THE comic store or at the Java Cup. She wasn't at any of the places she usually hangs out.

I lock my bike to a pole, then stand on the sidewalk looking at Sarah's house and the cop car sitting out front.

I know I have to go in there. I have to tell them about today. About how miserable Sarah looked. I don't know if they'll want me there, or if they'll think I'm intruding. But I have to do something.

Mrs. Meadows answers the door.

"Is Sarah back?" I ask, though I already know from the cop car that she's not.

Mrs. Meadows looks at me distractedly, her face too white, her lips almost bloodless. "No, she's not. I'm sorry—"

"Nick," I say.

"But this isn't a good time," Mrs. Meadows continues. She starts to close the door.

Before I know what I'm doing, I've rammed my boot in to

stop her. "Mrs. Meadows — please. I love your daughter. Maybe I can help."

Mrs. Meadows's face looks like it's going to crumple, but then she takes a breath, nods, and lets me in.

The house smells like a flower shop — like flowers and earth, and beneath that the faint scent of lemon floor polish. It smells clean, like Sarah does. Not like the stale, greasy scent of takeout food that's always at my place.

I hear voices — a deep rumble and a higher, frightened chatter. I follow Mrs. Meadows into the living room. Charlene's there, her arms around her wide tummy, talking to a cop. A man — it's got to be Sarah's dad — looks up at me with red-rimmed, intense eyes, his grief something I can almost taste.

"Who's this?" the officer asks abruptly.

Mrs. Meadows flaps her hands. "He's Sarah's boyfriend."

Charlene looks skeptical, and Mr. Meadows raises his eyebrow. I don't correct Mrs. Meadows — I want to be here. I want to help.

The officer makes a clicking sound with his tongue. "You know where she is?"

"No," I say, swallowing. *I wish I did.*

"When did you last see her?"

"Just after dismissal. She looked unhappy — like she did all day."

The officer swings back to Charlene. "You were the last one to see her — walking home with those boys after her."

My hands become fists. *Some boys were bullying Sarah again?* I should have walked with her, even if she didn't want me to. It takes everything I have to keep quiet and listen.

Charlene nods her head, her eyes big in her face.

The officer flips open his notebook and slowly, maddeningly, licks his fingers and turns the pages, reading silently. "Kirk, that right? The ringleader?" he asks Charlene.

"Yes," Charlene says faintly.

Mr. and Mrs. Meadows watch Charlene with such pained expressions that she must wish she were anywhere else.

"Last name?" the officer says.

"I told you, I don't know," Charlene says plaintively, her voice almost a whine. "He was new today."

The new guy, the one Charlene was hanging all over? He had something to do with this? No wonder Charlene looks scared. I'll kill her myself. She's supposed to be Sarah's best friend!

"Description?" The officer holds his pen in midair.

"Detective, you already went over this," Mrs. Meadows says, wringing her hands. "Don't you think you should be out there looking for Sarah?"

Yeah! Go find her! What if she's hurt and you're just wasting time standing around here talking to us?

"This is important, ma'am," the detective says. He turns to Charlene, whose legs are shaking. "Description?"

I close my eyes and pull up the times I saw the new guy

today. "Short, dark brown hair, sideburns, bangs that fall into his eyes. Dark, intense eyes, I think brown with some specks of yellow. High cheekbones, thin lips that tend to go into a sneer, narrow shoulders. Walks with a swagger. Black leather jacket, white T-shirt, blue jeans with a hole in the knee, black boots, like cowboy boots, that aren't meant for winter. Had an expensive-looking watch on his wrist. Oh, and his right eyebrow is pierced."

I open my eyes to see everyone staring at me. "I'm sorry, that's all I can remember," I say. "But I can draw him for you, if you like."

Wordlessly, the cop holds out his notebook and pen. I do a quick line drawing, then fill in more detail and add some shading. I draw the new boy smirking, his arm around a girl's shoulders. Her face doesn't fit in the space, and it's not important, anyway.

I hand the pad back to the cop, who whistles. "We sure could use you on our team when you get a bit older. You'd make a great sketch artist."

"Thank you, sir," I say. What I want to say is, "Why aren't you out there looking for Sarah?" But I know that he's just doing his job. Still, I feel a small glow of pride that my work might actually help find her.

The detective turns the pad around to Charlene. "This look right?"

She nods. "Nick got him perfectly." She glances at me. "You're as amazing as Sarah said you are."

Mr. and Mrs. Meadows crane their necks to see.

Sarah said I'm amazing? A smile almost breaks through my fear.

"Fine," the detective says. "After the boys left, I understand there was a man who offered Sarah a ride."

A man offered Sarah a ride? That is so classic! Why aren't they running this guy down right now?

"Yeah," Charlene says. "After he scared the boys away. But Sarah refused. And then it started sleeting, and I went home . . ." Charlene finishes miserably.

The cop clears his throat. "Can you describe the man again? Anything you can think of might help."

"Do you think he . . . did something to her?" Charlene asks, looking sick.

"It's important that we follow every lead."

What kind of half-assed answer is that? Has this guy ever looked for a missing girl before? My stomach churns as I realize that this is what Sarah is. Missing.

"I didn't see him very long," Charlene says. "And it was sleeting. But I think he had dark hair, and he looked like he worked out. He wore a suit."

"How old do you think he was?" the cop asks.

"Uh, not old, like you guys . . . I mean" — Charlene's rosy face grows sweaty — "he was maybe in his twenties."

That's her description? I stare at Charlene. No wonder the cop was impressed with my answer. *You can do better!* I urge her silently, but she doesn't add anything.

"I don't suppose you saw this guy?" the detective asks me hopefully.

I shake my head. "Sorry."

The detective sighs gustily. "Sound like anyone you know?" he asks Sarah's parents. Her mom shakes her head. Her dad scratches his cheek, looking unsure. I feel for them. With that description, it could be anyone.

"Do you know what make the car was?" the detective asks Charlene.

Charlene hesitates. "It was little. Not big like a station wagon or a van. And it was red. Or maybe orange or brown."

God. I know most girls aren't into cars, but you'd think she could describe it a little better. I grit my teeth, forcing myself to stay calm.

The cop reaches into his breast pocket and pulls out some business cards. He hands one to Charlene, one to me, and one to each of Sarah's parents. "You think of anything else, you call this number."

I slip the card into my back pocket.

Mr. Meadows touches Charlene's arm. "Thank you for telling us everything," he says hoarsely. "We appreciate your honesty."

Charlene looks up at him. "I should have said something. I should have stopped them —"

"Sarah's faced worse," Mr. Meadows says, then turns to the officer. "She'd never run away. She's put up with people being cruel about her face her entire life." His voice chokes off.

"You said she was upset this morning after your news," the detective says. "And she already had issues with her birthmark. Then those hoodlums followed her. That's a lot for anyone to deal with. I know you think it's not something she would do, but most parents don't until it happens."

Mr. Meadows looks like he wants to strangle the cop, but the cop continues, as if he doesn't notice. "At Sarah's age, with her hormones running wild, we have to rule out running away before we do anything else — unless we find information that tells us otherwise."

I raise my voice. "Sarah wouldn't run away."

Mr. Meadows smiles at me wanly.

"Yeah, she wouldn't," Charlene says. "It's not Sarah."

The detective frowns at Charlene and me. "Thank you for your cooperation today," he says, and I know he's telling us to leave.

"Let me know if you hear anything," I say to Mrs. Meadows, who nods. I turn and walk down the hall toward the door.

"Nick, wait!" Charlene calls, and runs after me.

We step out together into the cold night air. The door closes behind us, sounding final, somehow.

"You think they'll find her?" Charlene asks, her voice heavy.

"They'd better."

"You were right — she'd never run away."

"I know." I kick at the slush. "That cop doesn't know her."

Why did I wait to tell Sarah how I feel about her? If I never see her again, I'll regret that for the rest of my life. But it can't happen like that. It can't. I love her.

I run my hands through my hair and turn to Charlene. "Will you show me where you saw her last?"

"Why?" she asks, sounding suspicious, guilty, and sad, all at once.

I shrug. "I know it's stupid, but I can't just go home. I'm going to look for her."

Charlene straightens her shoulders. "Then I'm going, too. Come on. Maybe someone saw something."

My thoughts exactly.

"But Nick — if Kirk had anything to do with this, I'll never forgive myself."

I don't have anything to say to that.

Charlene starts down the street, hugging her coat to her, her head down, the wind whipping her hair into her face. I never thought we'd walk down the street together. We don't have anything in common, except that we both like Sarah. But now, at least, we've got the same goal in mind. Find Sarah, wherever she is.

SARAH

I TRY TO YANK the blindfold off, but it's as tight as if he nailed it into my skull. I reach up and explore the buckle at the back of my head — and touch a cold, hard lump of metal. It's a narrow rectangle with a **U** looped through a tiny hoop, where the finger of the buckle should be.

My breath falters. A padlock. He's *locked* the blindfold onto me. I feel for the chin buckle, but it's the same.

Holy shit! I yank the blindfold strap as hard as I can, over and over again, each yank jerking at my head until my neck aches and my arms get pins and needles from being raised above my head for so long. The lock is so little, it seems like I should be able to break it, but I can't.

I want to collapse on the floor and cry, but that won't get me out of here. I pound my thighs. How am I supposed to escape if I can't even see?

I grit my teeth. Blind people cope without sight every day. If they can do it, so can I.

I push myself off the wall and take one step, then another into the darkness, my hands shaking. It's scary to walk blind; I feel like I'm going to fall into some gaping pit.

I frown at myself. I'm being silly. I take another slow step forward, and cobwebs attach to my face — sticky, delicate tendrils. I shudder and swipe them off, then shuffle forward again.

My feet want to cling to the floor, drive my toes through the wood, while my legs want to run. I've got to hurry; he could come back anytime.

I take bigger, faster steps, my breath squeezing inside my chest. My hands slap against the cold wall. I feel lumpy plaster joining drywall, touch the bumpy hard ridges of nail heads.

I thrust my hands farther along the wall, and my fingers slam into raised, rough wood, splinters piercing my skin.

A door? But as fast as I hope, it's gone. The wood goes sideways, like a window frame. I move my hand up, but I touch only the roughness of boards, not the smooth coolness of glass. I feel for a gap, but there isn't one. He's blocked it off. I want to pound the boards, but instead I shove myself forward — and there it is. A door frame, then a door. *Thank you, god.*

I brush my hands over the grainy surface, searching for the doorknob, but there's no knob, no handle, nothing sticking out at all. Just a hole where the doorknob should be, cold wind whistling in. Not a neat, smooth hole, but a jagged hole, like it was hacked at with a knife. I thrust my fingers through and yank. The door doesn't move.

The crisp air streaming through the hole taunts me. I yank at the door harder, kick at it, pain stabbing my toes, tears soaking the blindfold. There has to be another way to open the door.

I feel the hinges, hoping there's something I can unscrew, but my fingers slide over unmoving metal. Screams tremble in my throat.

I whirl around and start along the next wall, feeling my way around the room. I count the walls as I go, but even so I have to go around three times before I can convince myself there's only the one door.

He plans to keep me here. Something snaps in my mind, and I go at the door like I'm crazed, slamming into it with my body, not caring about the way it jars my teeth, my bones, hurts my shoulder. I batter the door, clawing and kicking and screaming until I am sobbing with exhaustion.

I sink to the floor, trembling and feeling sick. I hurt all over, I have to pee, and I am intensely thirsty.

Don't let me die here. Please. I never got to say goodbye. Never got to tell Mom I'm sorry, tell Dad how lucky I am to have him for a father. A whimper wrenches its way out of my throat. I want to be with them so badly, I can almost feel Dad's strong hand on my shoulder, can almost smell Mom's orange-blossom perfume, the one Dad gave her when I was born.

I wonder if they're thinking of me right now, if they even know I'm missing; wonder if my fear and pain has somehow reached them. I know it's crazy thinking, but I want it to be true.

I want to be saved — *need* to be saved — the way people are in movies. The hero never giving up, breaking down the door or bursting through the wall to save the victim, sometimes at the last minute, but always, always succeeding.

Even more than that, I wish I were Superman or She-Hulk, so I could rip off my blindfold and smash my way out of here, bricks and bits of wood flying. But I'm just an ordinary girl locked up by some sicko.

I chew on my lip. If Brian is anything like the villains in comic books, he could be out there right now, watching me trying to escape, gloating at my defeat.

I leap to my feet and feel my way back to the door, then press my mouth to the hole. "Are you out there, you sick jerk? Are you listening? You haven't won, you hear me?" My voice is hoarse. "I'm going to get out of here! And when my dad finds out you did this — and he will — he's going to make sure you go to jail for a long time!"

I stop shouting and listen.

There's nothing, just silence. It was stupid to think he'd be watching. He probably left me here to die.

And then shoes crunch along the gravel and ice, pebbles jarring against one another.

SARAH

AT FIRST I THINK the footsteps are heading away from me, but then they get louder. I feel like I'm choking on my own heart.

The crunch of gravel stops. I strain to hear, my breath rasping in my throat.

"I won't be threatened," Brian says, his voice surprisingly close. "You'd better learn that fast. You've just guaranteed that your parents will suffer."

"What? No, please —"

But his footsteps retreat, leaving me alone.

I lean back against the door. He could be lying to get me to behave. But if he isn't . . .

I take a shuddering breath. If he isn't, I just put them in danger. God, I hope he's lying. *Please let him be lying.*

I leap up and pound the door again, pound it as hard as I can, kicking and punching and tearing at it, but it is just as unmovable as before.

I need to warn my parents — and I can't. I don't know what to do, except I have to stop thinking about it or I'll break. I really think I'll break, just start screaming and never stop.

I sink to my knees, my bladder aching. I can't believe I'm locked up here, all alone, waiting for a psycho to come back. If Brian fooled me — *me* with my great sense of people — then how will Dad and Mom ever figure out who kidnapped me? He's probably heading back there now to console them.

I slam my head against the door. If they can't see through him, then no one will know where I am. No one will know what happened to me.

SARAH

A BIRD BEGINS TO chirp like nothing's happened, an inane chirp that makes me want to scream.

I wrap my arms around myself and try to keep from losing it. The need to pee is getting worse. I can't believe I have to; not right now. I've got to escape! But how can I, when I can't even open the door? And there's no one around to find me even if I did. I know that now. Brian wouldn't have taken the chance of removing my gag if he thought someone could hear me scream. I must be far away from people. Very far.

I wonder if they've found my backpack yet. If Mom is crying over it, if Dad is pacing up and down the hall. I wonder if Charlene's instant messaged me, or if she even knows I'm missing.

I sniff back tears. There's no one in the world who knows where I am except Brian — and he's not going to tell. There's just him — and me. And no one will ever think to look at him. If they look at anyone, it will be Bad Boy. After what he did today, he's the most obvious suspect. All anyone will remember about Brian, if they think about him at all, is how he saved me. No one will ever find me.

No. I can't die in this shack. There's got to be something I can use to help me. Something he overlooked.

I get down on my hands and knees and slowly move forward, sweeping the floor with my hands. My fingers touch the stiff cotton, and I jerk my hand away and keep going in as straight a line as I can without being able to see — all the way to the wall. I repeat this until I've covered the entire room.

I lean my head back. There is nothing here except the down comforter. This is a holding tank, a prison. Nothing more.

I have to pee so badly now that it hurts. I shift uncomfortably. My abdomen, my crotch, even the muscles at the top of my thighs all hurt. There's nowhere to go, no toilet — and I am not taking my jeans off when he could be standing outside watching, waiting for me to make myself vulnerable. I've been trying to ignore the pressure, but the pain is getting bad.

I clench my fists. "I can control this. Mind over matter."

But the pressure builds, and I have to let go. I feel relief as warmth spreads across my jeans and down my legs, and the pain subsides.

And then I feel the cold, wet fabric against my legs. It's all I feel.

I haven't peed myself since I was little and got scared watching *Star Wars*. Mom cleaned me up and didn't even get mad. I want to hear her and Dad's voices so badly, want them to tell me it's okay, that I will get out of here.

I slide down to the floor. I need to cry, but I won't let myself give in. I think of Mom, of the way she's always so positive no matter how bad things get, and I draw that strength to me.

I *will* get out of here.

I'm starting to feel the cold in my toes and fingers, and deep in my core. I shudder. What's positive about my situation? There has to be something.

I guess I'm lucky I have shelter, that he didn't tie me up outside, and that he left me my down coat and the comforter. There. I can do this positive-thinking thing when I have to. I draw my knees up to my chest and hug myself, trying to keep warm.

But I'm not just cold. I'm fiercely thirsty. My mouth is so dry I can hardly swallow. I wish I had something, anything, to drink. Orange juice, root beer, chocolate milk — I want them all. Hot chocolate, tea — I'd even take coffee, though I hate its bitter taste. I can't believe I actually stood in the grocery store last week and argued with Mom over which brand of juice to buy. Right now I'd take anything, even the store brands that never taste as good. I try not to swallow.

I read once that a person can go for forty days without food, but only seven days without water. I can't have been here for more than a few hours, but I'm so thirsty my tongue is stuck to the roof of my mouth. I shouldn't be this thirsty; it must be the drug he gave me. But telling myself that doesn't help.

Anything's better, though, than him being here. Unless he's left me here to die. But what's the point of kidnapping me just to let me die?

I shiver. He had to kidnap me for a reason. Ransom? But my parents aren't rich, and Brian knows Dad's company is in trouble. So why? To rape me? To kill me?

I gag. Those are the most likely answers. But then why didn't he do it already?

I hate not knowing why Brian did this. But I don't really want to know, either. I just want to escape.

It doesn't make sense. None of this makes sense. I trusted Brian. So did my parents. But here I am, Brian's prisoner. And Dad and Mom? They must be crazy with worry.

I miss them so badly. And I'm scared for them. Scared for me, too. But I can't do anything until Brian gets back. That's when things will change. I'll *make* them change. Because he'll have to open the door to come inside. And when he does, I will burst out of this prison.

I rest my head on my knees and wait.

NICK
7:50 P.M.

I CAN'T BELIEVE WHAT a prick Charlene's dad is. I could hear him swearing at her right through the phone, telling her to get her fat ass home. I felt sorry for her, though I tried not to show I'd heard.

I wish she'd stayed. It's cold, lonely work stopping passersby to ask them if they've seen Sarah, going into stores and asking shopkeepers who don't want to talk to me once they see I'm not buying anything. I worry that I'm wasting my time, that there's something else I should be doing to find her, but I don't know what.

I trip. I look to see what snared me — and stop breathing. I recognize that She-Hulk badge. I take a step back and nudge the backpack with my foot, turning it over and scooting it closer to a streetlight to be sure.

It's Sarah's, all right. The little Superman figure dangling from the zipper pull, the Wonder Woman button I gave her, the

Batgirl badge she made herself so that it would be her favorite Batgirl, Cassandra Cain . . .

I think I'm going to be sick. Sarah would never leave her bag. I know for sure now — something bad has happened. If only I'd walked her home, or convinced her to go to the comic store with me. If only I'd been with her.

God. I close my eyes. I don't want it to be true.

I look again. It's still lying there in a dark, sodden lump.

I feel surreal staring at her bag, like it's not really there or I'm not really here, but I know it is and I know I am. I wake my cell and call the detective, telling him what I found. I hang up and can't remember a thing he said. I just know he's coming.

I pray that Sarah isn't lying in a ditch somewhere. Pray that she's still alive.

I lean over, trying not to puke. I have to let Sarah's parents know. I swipe open the keypad on my cell and call directory assistance.

Mrs. Meadows stands shaking over Sarah's backpack. Mr. Meadows curses and turns away. The detective's already taped off the area, and two more cop cars have pulled up, their lights flashing silently.

I hover in the background. I feel like a dirty voyeur watching their pain and grief, but I can't look away. I need to know what happens.

A cop leaning over the gutter cries out, bags something, and holds it up. I move closer. A cell phone in a Wonder Woman skin. Sarah's cell phone. Mrs. Meadows runs over.

"Now, Mrs. Meadows, you know you can't touch it," the detective says. "We need it for evidence."

Mrs. Meadows whirls around, her fists clenched, and for a second I think she's going to punch him. "What are you doing to find her? Tell me what you're doing!"

I take a cautious step forward. I want to know, too.

"We've questioned that boy who bullied Sarah; he alibis out. So we're tracking down new leads. We've put out an AMBER alert for Sarah. We're getting roadblocks in place as we speak. Sarah's description and photo have been sent to police stations around the country, and we've got people patrolling the roads. We're doing everything we can to find her."

"Too little, too late," Mr. Meadows says, rounding on the detective, his face haggard. "You should have been out looking for her hours ago! Who knows how much time has been wasted."

"And it's not enough," Mrs. Meadows says. She draws herself up taller, her face as pale as the snow. "I want us on every TV station, radio station, and newspaper that will have us. Websites, too. We've got to get the word out, appeal to whoever did this to Sarah." She glares up at the detective. "Can you arrange that?"

The detective looks humbled. "Yes, ma'am, I can."

"Good," Mrs. Meadows says, nodding sharply. "Then do it."

I see where Sarah gets her brassiness from.

The cop walks a few steps away, signaling to another officer talking on a radio.

I edge closer, my throat dry. "Mrs. Meadows, Mr. Meadows—I want to help find Sarah. I'm good with computers. If you let me, I can set up a website with her photo, and ask people to send in tips. And I can put posters up in the neighborhood and at school. Maybe someone saw something that will help us get her back."

Mr. Meadows rubs a shaking hand across his eyes. "I design for a living. I can do the poster and get one of my team to do the website, but I'd sure appreciate your help—especially if you can get the bare bones up tonight. And you probably know more social networks to reach out to than we do."

"I'll get on it right away."

Mrs. Meadows squeezes my hand. "Thank you, Nick. Come by anytime tonight, no matter what the hour. We'll be up." She smiles painfully.

I'm surprised she remembers my name.

"Why don't you just come work at our house?" Mr. Meadows says. "That is, if it's all right with your parents."

"It'll be okay with my dad," I say, my voice hoarse.

Mr. Meadows nods, then walks to their car and opens the back door. "Then hop in."

Hang on, Sarah. We're going to find you.

SARAH

I CAN'T STAND THE stink of my own urine, the roughness of my jeans where I peed. I find my way to the door and shake it as hard as I can, but it is as firm and as unyielding as a wall. I don't think I'm going to get out of here alive. I wish I hadn't brushed Nick off this morning. Wish I hadn't fought with Mom. Wish I'd told Dad how much I loved him, how nothing mattered as long as we were all together. There are so many things I would have done differently if I'd known today would be my last day.

No.

I can't think like that. I'm going to get out of here. And when I get back home, I will do the things I wish I'd done.

I shiver, my teeth chattering. I don't want everything to end like this. *I don't want to die.* I slide to the floor and crawl across, patting in front of me until I find the comforter. I wrap it around me, up to my nose, trying to get warm.

— — —

A sound jolts me awake. I sit up stiffly, clutching the comforter around me tighter. There's a scrape of metal on metal, the thud of something moving aside.

I leap to my feet and turn to face the sound, my legs trembling.

The door opens, bringing a rush of cold air. The stench of Brian's pine cologne assaults my nostrils.

I charge toward the breeze, the sounds — and slam into a hard, lumpy protrusion, and then a warm body.

Brian grunts. Something heavy thuds to my feet, the floor reverberating. Brian grips my shoulders. "Where do you think you're going?"

"Let me go!" I wrench away and try to get past him.

Brian jerks me back. "This is your new home, Sarah. Get used to it. And let me tell you, you've got it better than the others did, so quit your victim act. I know you're stronger than they were."

Others. Bile rises in my throat. I swallow it back. There was more than one. "What happened to them?" I ask, trying to keep my voice from shaking.

Brian shoves me back farther, one foot nudging something along the floor, making a scraping noise. The door slams shut. "I gave them freedom from the pain in their lives — the same way I'll give it to you."

"I don't need that! I'm happy. Just let me go home."

"You didn't look happy yesterday when those boys were taunting you. I'll bet you would have gone straight to your mommy, crying your eyes out, wanting her to make it all better. And your poor mother would have been crying along with you." His voice cracks. "That's not happy, Sarah. Not for you, and not for anyone around you. But I can give you happiness. I can give you freedom from your pain."

"I don't need freedom. Mom says that pain makes us stronger."

"She *would* say that. She has to reassure you, and herself, too. It's how she gets through the pain you cause her."

"Just let me go home. I won't tell anyone."

"Sorry, no can do," Brian says cheerfully.

It almost sounds like he cares about my mom. I bite my lip. "If you keep me here, you're not just hurting me; you're hurting my mom and dad, too."

"You're the one who's hurting them." He takes hold of my hands, his skin soft, like he uses hand cream. I try to yank away, and he squeezes my hands tighter, my bones grinding together. "Your parents can't look at you without suffering."

"And that's *my* fault?" God, he's already got me believing him. I've got to stay with my own reality. "They love me. Not knowing where I am is what will make them suffer."

"That will fade. And then they will feel better — a whole lot better. They will know freedom, too." He lets go of my hands. "I brought you some food."

My stomach growls loudly. I want to punch it into silence.

Brian laughs.

I clench my teeth, hating that he knows I'm hungry. Hating that he is here. I back up into a wall. The room feels too small with him in it.

"You see? I tend to your needs. I am merciful—more than your parents have ever been."

I turn my stained cheek away from his voice and lick my dry, rough lips. *He's crazy. He's crazy, and I never saw it.*

"You thirsty? You must be. Do you want something to drink?"

I want to refuse him, but my throat aches too much. "Please."

"Good. You can have something, then. I'm not unreasonable."

"Then let me go."

Brian doesn't answer. There's the sound of a zipper, then a cap unscrewing and liquid being poured into a cup. He holds the cup to my lips, and it shakes, or maybe I'm the one shaking.

I gulp at the water, trying to drink it all before he takes it away. The strap pinches my throat and water dribbles over my chin and down my neck, but I don't care; it tastes so sweet and good.

He takes the cup away.

"No! Please. Not yet."

"You'll give yourself cramps if you drink too fast," Brian says. "Just wait a minute."

His voice is almost tender. I don't understand how he can sound like that. He's a monster.

"Are you hungry?" Brian asks. "Think you could eat something?"

Saliva fills my mouth. I want to gobble down whatever he offers me, but I know I can survive without it. And the gentleness in his voice feels wrong now, put on, like he's trying to make me trust him.

"Are you hungry or aren't you?" he asks, anger creeping into his voice.

Anger is good. That means he isn't getting what he wants. "Thirsty."

Brian grunts. I hear water splash into the cup, and then he holds the cup to my lips again.

I drink until I can't drink any more, and then I take a few more swallows. When he fills the cup for the fourth time and puts it to my lips, I turn my head away.

"Fine," Brian says. He doesn't sound angry this time.

I feel him move closer, the heat from his body pushing against me. I wish I could see him. Wish I knew what he was doing.

"You peed yourself. I'd better clean you up."

"That's okay! Don't bother."

Brian snorts. "Don't be a prude." He unbuttons my jeans.

I hit out wildly. "Don't touch me!"

He grips my wrists. "Don't be like that. I want to help you. Can't let you sit around smelling like that."

Down goes the zipper of my jeans. He pushes my T-shirt up, then rests his hands on my hips.

My skin ripples. *Don't let this be happening.*

He yanks at my stiff jeans.

"Get off me!" I claw at him, but he doesn't stop, just keeps tugging my jeans down. I wish I'd never bought my new, cutesy undies, bright blue low-rises with red trim and SUPERGIRL printed on them in sparkly silver. I wanted to feel strong after the pain of my first treatment. Like I was wearing armor no one could see.

Brian yanks at my undies.

I kick and punch him, but it's like I'm not doing anything.

"I've waited longer for you than the other girls — but I can wait only so long. You have to know what love is."

"This isn't love! This is rape." I punch him again.

"No, Sarah — this is love. Now, will you let me teach you?"

I scream from the pit of my stomach, as loud as I can.

He catches my wrists again, pressing so hard it hurts. "I'm not going to hurt you. But quit screaming, or I'll have to put the gag back in."

I can already feel it choking me. I strangle my voice into silence, his overpowering cologne tasting bitter in my mouth.

"You didn't give me your answer, you know," he says, his voice gentle.

No! I almost scream. *Get off me!* But I don't scream anything. I'm afraid he'll put the gag back in.

"Silence is understood to mean yes," he says.

Not with me, it isn't.

I hear water dripping, and then a wet cloth rubs over my leg, smelling like Ivory soap. Clean and pure.

I tremble as he works on my left leg, then my right. I can almost imagine I'm little again, Mom cleaning me up in the bathroom. I want it to be her.

And then he puts the cloth between my legs.

I jerk away, but he yanks me back, then pulls me to the duvet, the floor hard beneath it.

"No, no, stop!"

He straddles me, using his weight to keep me still. "Just relax."

I try to heave him off, and he sits on me harder.

There is the crinkle of a wrapper, and I can feel him fumbling beside me.

My teeth chatter. I know what he's doing.

At least I won't have to worry about him getting me pregnant an inane part of my brain thinks.

I claw at him, my nails scraping against his warm flesh, catching on his shirt, popping a button.

He slaps my face. "Stop that."

"No!" I shout, my voice breaking.

He pins my arms down and thrusts his way in. I can feel my flesh tearing.

Let it be over. Please, god, let it be over.

I bite him, getting hold of his cheek, then his ear, but he just moves faster, as if he likes my reaction.

Hot tears and snot burn against my skin.

All I can smell is him, his musky body odor and stinging cologne. His salty taste is in my mouth, sweat mixed with my tears. And it hurts. God, it hurts. "Get off me!"

His hands squeeze my throat, gripping tightly.

I can't breathe.

This is it. This is how I'm going to die. *I love you, Daddy.* My chest burns.

Brian shudders on top of me, then lies there, gasping, his hands leaving my throat.

I suck in air, his weight flattening my chest, making it hard to breathe. I am crying, choking and shaking and crying.

He heaves himself off me and strokes my cheek with his hand, his fingers catching on the blindfold. "You'll come to like it, Sarah; you'll see."

Go to hell. But I don't say that. I know he'd only enjoy it.

I lie there, rigid, tears leaking from my blindfolded eyes, until his hand leaves my face and he pulls away.

I hear him stand, brush off his suit, zip up his pants, his breath heavy.

I try to make my body part of the floor, stiff and unfeeling, as he crouches over me and kisses my forehead.

"I'll see you soon," he whispers.

No!

He walks away, footsteps creaking. The door squeaks open, then thuds closed. There's a grating sound, then silence.

I pull my knees up to my chest, tuck my face against them, and try to rock the pain away.

SARAH

I ROCK MYSELF BACK and forth, back and forth. I can almost feel the way my dad used to rock me when I was little. I wish he were here now, holding me. I want to press my head against his shoulder and make this all go away.

Pain drones between my legs. I touch my fingers to my sore skin and feel hot, sticky wetness. Blood.

I shudder, my stomach heaving.

I feel so dirty, like his smell is clinging to me still, sweat and cologne and sex. Like he's stained me deeper than my birthmark ever could. Stained my soul, stained everything that makes me who I am.

I scrub at my skin, trying to get rid of the feeling of his body against mine, but it stays like an imprint in my flesh. I hate my body, hate what it remembers, what it let him do.

No. It's him I should hate.

I reach for my clothes, patting the floor until I find them.

Undies first. I ease them up over me, breathing out at the pain. Then my damp jeans, one leg at a time, biting down on my lip. It doesn't matter if it hurts. I won't let him find me without my jeans on.

I pull them all the way on, do up the zipper, fumble with the button. I feel safer already, as if wearing my jeans will somehow keep him from raping me again. As if they did anything to stop him just minutes ago.

I retch and try to slam the memory out of my mind.

I get unsteadily to my feet. Why has he left me here again? If he's going to kill me, why doesn't he just get it over with? Or does he want to keep me here forever? But that can't be right, not if he's had other girls. My stomach heaves again, hot acid rushing up my throat. I bend over, gagging and spitting.

I've got to escape.

I yank at the blindfold, but it's buckled so tightly, it's like it's become part of my skin. "Why'd you leave this stupid blindfold on if you were going to untie everything else?" But I know why. It keeps me helpless.

I go over what I know: the door is locked from the outside, the windows are boarded up, and I don't have any tools. And Brian might kill me when he comes back.

No. I'm missing something. I press my hands to my head. That thud I heard earlier, the dragging sound.

I force myself across the uneven floor, sweeping each foot in front of me until it hits something. I bend down and touch stiff, hard fabric, a long zipper, short handles. A sports bag, the kind jocks carry to football and hockey practice. Inside is roughened, itchy fabric. I explore it with my fingers. A wool hat. What an odd thing to give me. I reach in again, my fingers touching a small folded rectangle. I open it up, the plastic crinkling loudly. It's a strong, thin plastic blanket, bigger than me. I sit there, feeling it between my fingers. It reminds me of the survival blanket Dad used to pack when we went camping. I sit back on my heels.

Brian wants me to survive the cold. To survive more than just a few hours. My heart pounds so hard it feels like it's going to burst. I take a slow breath to calm myself. I wrap the blanket around my shoulders like a cape, tying it at my neck, then reach inside the bag again, touching cold, smooth plastic, plastic that is pear shaped and has a handle. I run my fingers to the top of the plastic and twist. The cap comes off in my hand.

I sniff it. No smell. Heft it up with both hands and take a small, careful mouthful. It tastes cool and clear. Fresh.

Water. He's left me water. I swallow, then swallow again, feeling the liquid trickle down my throat, easing the soreness. I can't use the thin plastic as a tool, but the water will keep me alive.

My hands tremble beneath the heaviness of the jug. It feels bigger than a jug of milk.

I choke. "He's not coming back soon. Maybe not ever."

I screw the lid back on the jug and set it down at my feet. It probably holds at least three days' worth of water — more, if I'm careful. It'll take me at least that long to work on the window. *Damn him.*

What else did he leave me? I reach toward the bag, almost dreading what I'll find. I touch a bucket. No, two of them. One tucked inside the other.

"Now, why did he give me . . . ?" I smell the stink of urine on my jeans, and I know. I know, even though I don't want to.

I feel the bucket carefully with my fingers. Hard, rounded plastic, no sharp edges. If I broke it, could it be used as a tool? A weapon?

I feel the bucket again. It's not heavy enough to defend me, and the plastic wouldn't be strong enough to use as a lever beneath the boards.

I push them both away and delve further into the bag, touching, smelling, and opening everything. There's a box of crackers, seven bananas. A jar of peanut butter, a stack of flimsy drinking glasses, and two more jugs of water. Enough for a week.

Is he going to leave me here an entire week? I hear screaming in my mind. Screaming that starts so deep inside me that if I let it, it will blot everything else out, even my own thoughts. I press my palms against the floor and try to breathe normally. He's planned this so carefully. Made sure there was nothing I could use.

But I can't give up. I won't.

I rest one hand on the bag. I know I should figure out a plan, or try breaking down the door again. But I feel weak and shaky, my stomach hollow, and the scent of the ripe bananas makes it hard to concentrate. My stomach clenches, demanding to be fed.

"Fuck it all!"

I grab a banana, rip off the peel, and stuff big pieces into my mouth. It tastes fresh and clean, not like this room. Not like Brian.

I swallow it down, almost choking in my eagerness. And then it's gone.

It doesn't even begin to fill my hunger. Before I know what I'm doing, I've unscrewed the lid to the peanut butter and torn the foil seal completely off, and am scooping the nutty mixture out with my fingers. Its thick, smooth sweetness wraps around my tongue.

Heaven.

I cram in more sticky sweetness. It glues my mouth together like cement. I almost choke on the peanut butter, trying to swallow it down. *Slower, I have to eat slower,* I tell myself, but I can't. I take a long gulp of cool water, and then I am tearing open the package of crackers and digging them into the peanut butter, cramming them in my mouth as fast as I can swallow. I'm like a starved dog gobbling its food without breathing, and I know I've got to stop so I don't just vomit it up again, got to stop so there will be some for later, but it's like my stomach has total control over me. I keep eating and drinking until I'm so full it hurts. Only then does my stomach release me.

I groan and wrap my arms around my too-tight stomach. It was frightening being so out of control, as if I were pure animal. I'm glad no one could see.

I reach for the peanut butter and feel down inside the jar. I've finished off almost half of it and most of the crackers. The bottle of water is a lot lighter, too.

In one meal I've eaten almost a third of all my food. "I've got to be more careful! I have to make it last until he gets back." I shake my head. "No. Until I get out of here."

If I get out of here.

But I won't let myself think that way.

I won't need it that long. I'll be out of here before he gets back. Still, I arrange what's left of the food into six piles, one for each day. One banana. Three crackers. And the half jar of peanut butter, the two and a half jugs of water. It doesn't seem like enough, but I can't imagine stretching it out any further. And surely someone will have found me by then.

I wipe my mouth with the back of my hand. I keep smelling him on me. I wish I could use some of the water to wash him off, but it's more important to drink it and stay alive.

Something scratches inside the walls. The mice. Or rats. They probably smell my food.

I set the piles of food into the bag and zip it up. I'm not letting some rodent eat what little I have. I feel for the jug to make sure the cap is on. My survival depends on it. If only I could see . . .

I reach for the blindfold again and tug. No matter how strong the leather is, it has to break sometime. If I go at it every day . . .

No. Someone will find me.

I wonder what my parents are doing right now. I imagine Dad pacing up and down the hall, yelling into his phone, urging the police to find me, imagine Mom calling around to all my friends, the school, trying to discover who saw me last. Charlene's one of the first people she'll call, so that should get her on the trail pretty quickly. And nothing can stop an angry, protective mother bear from finding her cub.

I unscrew the water, lift the heavy jug to my lips, and take another swallow. It feels so good going down my throat, cool and soothing, washing away the dryness, the thick sweetness left from the peanut butter —

I'm doing it again! Drinking away my ration.

I shove the water away from me, hear it thunk to the floor, hear the water glub out. I reach for it, patting. "No!" My hands slap water. I grab the jug and turn it upright, but it feels light, too light and empty.

Help me, Dad!

NICK
DAY 2, 8:30 A.M.

THE MEADOWSES WERE ON every channel I turned on last night. I watched them plead with whoever took Sarah to bring her home safely, Mr. Meadows looking like he could hardly stand up, Mrs. Meadows crying silently the entire time. But still we managed to get the poster designed and printed out, and the website up.

My eyes burn. I can't look away from Sarah's face on the poster. Her eyes are so sad. I wish I could strangle whoever first made her retreat from the world. Well, maybe press a rewind-and-redo button. Hell, I could use one of those myself. I'd make sure Mom never got into her car that night. I'd make sure Dad never lost his own mom. And I'd walk Sarah home every day, make sure she stayed safe.

I've already put up at least a hundred posters in the neighborhood, but I figure there might be someone from school who saw what happened. I staple Sarah's poster to the library bulletin board next to a Found poster for a dog and a chess club announcement. I'm going to put it up everywhere I can think of. Maybe even start slipping it through locker slats, or pasting it on the sides of lockers. I don't care if I get into trouble; finding Sarah is more important.

"Sarah's missing?" a girl asks.

Isn't that what the poster says? I want to snap. I turn. Gemma's looking at me earnestly. I bite back my anger. "Yeah. You seen her?"

Gemma shakes her head. "Not since yesterday."

"Yesterday when?"

"School."

"Yeah." My shoulders slump. I know it's a slim chance that anyone will know anything, but I have to try.

"You want help?"

"Sure." I hand her half my posters. I can always get more. "Make sure they go up where people can see them."

"Du-uh." Gemma rolls her eyes. "Don't worry. I can already think of a perfect place — over the tampon dispensers in the girls' bathrooms. No way they'll miss that."

My cheeks heat up. But she may have a point. Any way that we can get people's attention helps. "Thanks. I think something really bad happened to her."

Gemma's eyes grow softer. "I'm sorry. She's a real nice girl.

Doesn't seem right, bad things happening to good people, does it? If it had to happen to anyone, it shoulda been one of those mean bitches, like Madison."

"Yeah." Sadness is like a weight on my chest. "But it never seems to work out that way. Not often, anyway."

"Too true." Gemma looks at me for a moment, then squeezes my arm. "Hang in there, boy. I bet she'll make it. She don't look tough, but she is on the inside, where it counts."

I straighten. "You're right," I say, and staple another poster up.

Keep fighting, Sarah. Wherever you are.

SARAH

I'M GOING TO GET out of here. That's what I tell myself. I have to, or the terror and grief will make me give up. And I can't. I won't. I have a life to go back to, people who love me. People I love. I just have to get through until help comes, or until I can break free.

I keep seeing Dad's and Mom's faces, Charlene's . . . and Nick's. Nick's hurt face nags at me. I hug myself. I wish I'd ignored Madison's laughter and accepted *Ghostopolis*. Wish I'd spent more time with Nick. We have so much in common — our love of superheroes, our not fitting in, our desire to make our own comics someday. It hurts to think that I added to his feeling of being an outsider. I don't want that to be the last thing he remembers me for.

But I won't let it be. I plan over and over how I'll rush past Brian when he comes back, how I won't let him catch me this time.

No matter what I'm doing, I keep an ear out for signs of

people — for voices, footsteps, the sound of cars or laughter or music. I never hear anything human — just birds and the wind in the trees. But that doesn't stop me from trying to get help. At regular intervals I walk to the hole in the door, take a deep breath, and scream as loud as I can. Scream from the pit of my belly all the way up. I've never screamed so loud in my life. And then I stand there and listen — listen so hard it seems like my ears should bleed. But I never hear anything new.

Part of me thinks that's a good thing. At least Brian hasn't come back. I can't bear to think of him touching me again. Even the thought of his voice makes me want to gag. But another part of me is so afraid no one will come, not even Brian, and that I'll die here, alone.

I can't stop dreaming about the police rushing in to save me, or my dad, my mom, even Charlene. Charlene saw Brian; she has to have told the police. I imagine them following Brian here, then breaking down the door to get me, Dad folding me into his chest, Mom crying happy tears. I imagine it so vividly, so completely, that I almost hear their voices, and when I realize they're not really here, I want to weep. But Diamond would never cry. So I feel my way to the boarded-up window and try to find something I missed — a weak spot, a way out of here. I tug at the boards until my fingers burn with pain. And then I find myself slipping into the daydream again. The daydream of escape.

NICK
DAY 3, 3:20 P.M.

I CAN'T STOP THINKING about Sarah. I dream about rushing in to save her, and her throwing herself into my arms, hugging me tight, her happy tears wetting my neck. And then our kiss, full of relief and, later, passion. I know it's just a daydream, but it's so much better than my other thoughts. My worst-case scenarios that I can't stop picturing.

I've already bargained with god, with any possible deity out there, and offered anything I can think of, just as long as we get Sarah back safe. A part of me watches my crazed thoughts and scoffs. I've never believed in god or a creator or anything bigger than us. But I pray, anyhow. I'll do anything if it will help get Sarah back alive.

Mr. and Mrs. Meadows are still giving interviews with anyone who will have them, but I can tell the reporters are losing interest. It's been two days since Sarah went missing, and they haven't found anything new. One reporter said that if the police don't find a lead in the first forty-eight hours, it's unlikely we'll ever see that missing person again. I don't know how he could talk about Sarah like she's a statistic. But I'm not giving up hope. I can't. It would be like giving up on her.

Sarah's face was on a gossip rag today, the kind my mom used to read. It punched the breath right out of my lungs, seeing her sad, fierce eyes staring out at me. They printed a bunch of garbage about her — that she's a problem teen and a high risk as a runaway because of her low self-esteem and because she was bullied — but the crap they wrote doesn't matter. None of it does, as long as we get Sarah back.

My dad insisted I go to classes today, so I went, but I don't know what the point was. I couldn't do anything but think of Sarah.

She's got to be alive. I need her. She doesn't know it, but I do.

I trudge up to the Meadowses' house and knock on their door. Mr. Meadows answers, looking haggard, his eyes hollow, his cheeks stubbly, his clothes all rumpled like he hasn't slept or changed since Sarah went missing. He probably hasn't.

"Nick." Mr. Meadows forces a smile.

"Got more posters?" I ask, trying to sound hopeful, like we'll actually find her. It's getting harder to believe.

Mr. Meadows rubs a hand through his hair. "You bet. Come on in. You know where they are."

I pass by the kitchen. Mrs. Meadows is sitting at the table

staring into her coffee, her hair stringy and unwashed. A man sits with her at the table, leaning forward, talking to her in a hushed voice. Mrs. Meadows looks up when I pass but doesn't seem to see me.

"Hi, I'm Brian," the man says, holding out his hand. "Mr. Meadows's assistant. You're one of Sarah's friends, aren't you?"

"Yeah," I say, shuffling my feet. I want to be more than a friend. So much more. *Sarah, come home.*

"You're a good kid to help out like this. You must care about her a lot," Brian says, studying my face.

I can feel all the blood rush into my head. "I do." But I can't talk about it to some guy I don't even know, even if he is Mr. Meadows's assistant.

I go into the dining room where the stacks of boxes are and open one up. Sarah's face looks back at me. For a moment all I can see is the vivid purple-red stain on her cheek. She'd hate knowing that her face is plastered all over the city for everyone to gawk at. But if it'll get her back, I'm willing to risk her anger.

I grab a bunch of posters, as many as I can carry, and shove them into my backpack.

Brian pats Mrs. Meadows's shoulder and stands. "I'll help you put those up," he says, picking up a box. "We can cover a lot more ground in my car."

"Can you fit my bike in your trunk?" I ask.

"Sure can."

"Then it's a deal."

"Think you can find any place that doesn't already have one up?" Mr. Meadows says. "I plastered the area again last night."

I hear the false cheeriness in his voice. "With the two of us going at it, we're sure to," I say. "You never know. Someone might have seen her."

"Thank you," Mr. Meadows says, his voice breaking. "You've been a real trouper in all this."

I nod, then get out of there before we both start bawling again. Brian follows behind me.

SARAH

I WONDER IF THEY'RE still looking for me. If they've stuck my photo on one of those Missing posters I used to see, splashed my face on milk cartons, or put it up on a site for missing children. It feels weird to think of strangers knowing my name or recognizing my face all because Brian took me.

But I *am* a missing person. I'm missing from my life. I hope someone saw Brian take me, hope they track him until he returns here, leading them to me. But Brian was careful. I realize that now. He had it all planned out. Probably the only one who saw him was Charlene. Charlene and those boys. And what they would have seen was Brian *protecting* me.

Coldness spreads through my stomach. What if Brian told the police some story about me to mislead them? He's just calculating enough to do that. Then they might never find me. There's no one to tell them any different.

If I had my cell phone, I would be free by now. Even though

I don't know where I am, they could trace the signal and find a way to rescue me. But I have nothing. No way of reaching anyone.

Fear smothers my breath.

I force myself to my feet and start working on the window boards again. I will not let myself cry. I will not let myself give up hope. It hasn't been that long yet. There's still a chance someone will find me . . .

NICK

I BIKE MY WAY over to the police station, trying not to puff as I go. I started biking to help me slim down—I thought that would give me more of a chance with Sarah—but so far it hasn't helped me lose any weight. What it does do is make me sweat like a horse and make my face get red and blotchy. A real bonus.

I head to the front desk, suddenly nervous, and pull out the card the cop gave me. "Can I talk to Detective . . . Anderson, please?"

The cop behind the desk squints at me. "What's it about? You got an appointment?"

"It's about Sarah Meadows. Her disappearance."

"Wait there," the guy says, pointing at some chairs as he picks up the phone.

The detective comes bustling in a minute later, then stops when he sees me. "You got something you forgot to tell me?"

I stand. "No, sir. I just wanted to know if you've gotten any leads."

The detective rubs his face tiredly. "Look, kid — even if I had, I couldn't discuss them with you. I could only discuss them with Sarah's parents."

"No leads at all?" I say, my voice cracking.

"Kid, I told you —"

"I know, I know," I say. "But you're still looking, right? You've got to find her!"

The detective sighs. "We're doing what we can. We care about this just as much as you do."

"I doubt that."

"But we can't make miracles happen."

"Can you make *anything* happen?" I mutter.

"What?" the detective says, taking a step toward me, his bushy brows drawing together.

I can't believe I said that out loud. "I'm sorry. But Sarah's been gone only three days, and no one seems to care anymore."

"We care. We haven't given up," the detective says wearily. But his voice says something else.

"Then prove it. Find her." I turn and leave.

When I get outside I yank a chocolate bar from my bag and rip off the wrapper, cramming a big, gooey piece of chocolate, nougat, and caramel into my mouth. I don't know what I was hoping for, going there — that they'd have some big break in the case and let me know? I was dreaming. But every minute I'm not doing something to find Sarah feels like a waste.

I go to take another bite of my chocolate bar, but I've already finished it. I've been doing that a lot since Sarah disappeared, more than I used to. If I keep this up, Sarah's going to come home to an even more overweight me.

I sigh and check the website again from my phone, hoping someone's spotted Sarah. But there's nothing except comments from people expressing their sympathy or shock — comments from girls who tormented her every day and made her life hell. Comments from boys who never once looked her way except to stare at her cheek or heckle her. And comments from strangers suggesting that she could be a runaway — like they know her at all. To most of the kids at school, Sarah is just gossip, not a real person who's in trouble. I glare at them in the halls, but they don't notice, or if they do, they look startled, like they don't understand my anger.

I put Sarah's disappearance on all the sites, social networks, and chat groups I could think of, asking for people to keep their eyes open. People said they will, but I wonder how much time they'll take out of their own lives to give a thought to yet another missing girl.

I've asked everyone she knows when they last saw her — anyone she's ever talked to, even the ones who bullied her. But no one saw her after her confrontation with Kirk and Charlene. It's like she vanished. But someone's got to have seen something; I just have to find the right person.

Charlene and I have sat together at lunch every day since Sarah disappeared, and today Gemma joined us. It's almost a comfort, sitting with people who care about Sarah. And when I make my rounds after school to ask if anyone can remember anything, Charlene comes with me. I know she feels guilty about that day. I can see it all over her face. I wonder what she can read in mine. Desperation? Despair? Frustration? I don't want to know.

SARAH

I'VE BEEN TELLING MYSELF that it doesn't matter how long it's been. It doesn't matter that it's been five days since Brian left me here. But I know I'm fooling myself. Every day is another day missing from my life that I'll never get back. Every day is another day further away from my family, from the police, from anyone who might be able to find me. It's getting harder and harder to hope that someone will. I have to force myself to think positively, to keep the fear and despair from completely overwhelming me.

Each day feels so long. I hate the constant hunger, the never feeling full, the fierce thirst made worse by the sweet peanut butter and salty crackers, the weakness that runs through my body. I hate always feeling cold, even after I do jumping jacks and pace around the room as many times as I can bear, the thermal blanket tied around me. I hate sleeping on the hard, ungiving floor, and waking up so stiff and aching; it's as if I've grown old. But worse than that is the way I can't stop feeling his rough hands on my wrists, my throat, can't stop feeling him force himself into me. Can't stop wondering if today he's going to come back and do it all again — or worse.

I don't want to die. Thoughts about the other girls keep clawing themselves into my mind, both asleep and awake. Did Brian hold them prisoner like me? Did any of them get away? I try to hope, but I know, deep down, that they didn't. He wouldn't have let them.

Every day I pry at a board on the window, gripping the edges with my fingers, trying to loosen it — but it's like steel, unmoving. I work on the same one every time, hoping that the repetition will help it. Fear pushes me to pry at the board for longer and longer periods. My fingers are sore and bloody, stiff with cold, and it feels hopeless, but I can't stop, not for long.

I tug at the board again, put all my weight into it, wishing I could feel it give. If I do this hard enough, often enough, it's got to come loose sometime, doesn't it? I don't want Brian to come back, don't want to feel his hands on me again. And yet I want the water that he will bring. The food. I need it. Maybe, if I just do what he tells me to —

No. I won't go there.

I can't stop thinking about the rape, about how he enjoyed it more when I fought back. He likes overpowering me. Likes touching my stained cheek and making me react. So maybe next time I shouldn't react at all.

I yank on the board harder. I don't think I can let him put his hands on me without fighting back. But maybe that's a good thing. Maybe that's what's kept me alive. I don't really know why he hasn't killed me yet. I don't know what to do, except try to escape.

I lick my dry lips, trying to ignore the hunger that gnaws at me. I have only two piles of food left. Two little piles. And no way to replenish it. My stomach twists, begging to be filled.

I sink down, patting the uneven floorboards until I reach my stash. I wrap the quilt around me, then stuff two crackers into my mouth, letting their saltiness crunch against my teeth. I try to savor each mouthful, to be satisfied with what I have, but I want so much more. I swallow some water, washing the rough crumbs down. My stomach cramps hollowly. The rest of the food is sitting there, but I turn my face away. "I'm going to make it last."

I long for hot food to warm me from the inside and take away the chill that's always there. I need something filling to coat my stomach — Dad's chili, Mom's soup. I'd even take something from the school cafeteria. I just want something real — something that isn't crackers and peanut butter.

The stink of my sweat and urine nearly overpowers everything else, even the overripe bananas and the faint echo of Brian's cologne. My body odor wasn't so bad the first day. Even the second. I felt comforted by it. But now I smell like an animal, pungent and unwashed. It makes me feel dirty, which is probably how Brian wants me to feel. Maybe it'll turn Brian off so much he won't touch me anymore. Now not even Nick could look at me and find me beautiful, with my limp, oily hair, my urine-stained jeans, my cracked lips . . .

"If he ever really did." I'm not sure if he felt that way about me or if I imagined it. It was too hard to believe he could. I know what I look like; nobody ever lets me forget. But now I wish I'd at least paid more attention. If nothing else, Nick was offering me friendship. And I can always use another friend. It shouldn't have mattered that he's unpopular, chubby, and doesn't know how to dress well. He has a good heart; that matters more than any of those other things.

I shake my head. I chose to be blind. I knew Nick liked me. I could see it in his eyes. Even with my stained cheek, he liked me. But I wanted someone more popular than me, so I could feel better about myself. So I'd fit in. And that is the kind of behavior I hate in other people. Diamond would never act that way. She'd let herself love or be loved by anyone she wanted.

I pull the quilt around me tighter. I keep seeing the way Nick's eyes would light up when he caught me alone, like he was with someone special.

Like that day I stood up for Madison, before she got mean and thin. A crowd of girls, even some boys, were laughing at her, telling her she needed a garbage bag to hide her body. They called her metal mouth, fat blob, every name they could think of — and Madison just crouched there, hunched in on herself, her misery so visible.

Rage filled me then, puffing me up taller than I was. "You all think you're something, but you're not — not if you treat people this way!" I yelled. "Now back off!" They froze, all except Madison and Nick. Madison looked up at me, fat tears sliding down her blotchy face, her eyes grateful.

"Yeah! You cowards!" Nick yelled. That broke the others from their frozen states. Some swore at Nick or taunted him, but he held his ground next to me. I glared at them all, trying to emulate the frosty look Mom gave people who made stupid remarks about my cheek. "I feel sick looking at you all!" I screamed. "Go home!"

Some of the girls told me they were going to cut me up when I wasn't looking, but I just stood there, waiting them out. I forgot about my cheek, just felt the rage shimmering through me, like I could take them all down if I had to. I think they sensed that, because one by one they began to leave, until only Madison, Nick, and I were left.

Nick had always looked at me like I mattered. But that day it was like I was the sun — like I was all he could see. It felt good to have him look at me like that — like, for a brief moment,

I'd become Diamond, with her icy rage, sense of justice, and protectiveness for anyone who'd been hurt. I need that rage now. But even if I could draw on it, I have no one to turn it against but me.

Hunger claws at my stomach. I snatch up a banana and bite into its pulpy softness. The sweetness of it jolts my mind, waking me up a little. I know I'm getting used to this — to working on the boards, tugging the straps on the blindfold, walking to keep myself warm, and waiting for Brian to appear. Daydreaming about escape, remembering the people I love, drifting into sleep, and then trying the boards some more. Rationing out the food so carefully. And never showering, never changing my clothes, never doing any of the things I used to take for granted. My scalp itches.

I put the banana down, no longer hungry.

"I wish I knew why he's left me here so long. Does he think someone suspects him? Or does he want me to be afraid he won't come back?" I stand unsteadily, rest my hands against the wall, and start forward. I have to keep trying to escape. Have to keep believing I can. Or I'll just give up.

I pause at the door, the cold air stinging my fingers. "He wants me to be glad to see him. So if I'm not, will that keep me alive longer, or make him kill me faster?" God. I grip the hole in the door. I can't believe I'm even thinking about this.

There's a sharp crack, like a stick breaking.

Don't let it be him.

Another crack, then the rustle of bushes, the snap of twigs.

I put my lips to the hole. "Hello? Is someone there?"

My breath is coming so fast, I'm dizzy. I take a deep breath. "My name is Sarah Meadows. I'm trapped here! Please, help me!"

I stand there trembling, the banana heavy in my stomach. There is no sound, not even a branch breaking. And then the birds start up again with their relentless singing.

Screams erupt from me — loud, deep screams that startle the birds into silence, and I am glad.

I listen again, but there is no sound. I must have imagined it.

I need someone to rescue me. Need Dad and Mom to find me, need Charlene to have written down Brian's license plate, need a police officer to burst through this door. I need someone to hear my screams. But I know I am alone.

I find my way back to the window and start pulling on the board again. Charlene has to have told them what Brian looks like. And they must have put it together by now. I'll bet they're on their way to get me.

I shake the board as hard as I can. "Move, damn it!" But it's like it's part of the wall.

NICK

WE'RE HAVING AN ASSEMBLY about Sarah going missing to help the kids who are "distressed." Like anyone here cared about her that much, except Charlene and me, and maybe Gemma. Old Mr. Foster set up the assembly as if Sarah's dead. As if she's not coming back.

My eyes burn. I stare at the huge photo of Sarah that Old Fart-a-Lot Foster projected onto the gym wall. I refuse to listen to what they're saying. I know they're wrong.

Charlene looks like she's going to burst into tears any minute. Gemma looks pissed — like she doesn't like this any better than I do. And me — I'm just trying to hold it together and keep from screaming at people. All these people pretending Sarah meant something to them.

Some girls are sobbing, and some boys are all red in the face. I just look at them. They never even said hi to Sarah when she was around, unless it was to put her down. I look at the kids going over to talk to the counselor, and others leaning forward listening to Mr. Foster talk. I don't think they're faking what they feel — but I don't think it's just about Sarah, either. Maybe people are getting their own messed-up stuff out. Not intentionally, not in a mean way, but their emotions are spewing out, set off by Sarah's disappearance. Like Cindy over there, sobbing her face off. I remember now — she lost her little sister to cancer a year ago. Sarah disappearing — that's got to stir that up. And Tommy, his face too serious — his dad left them not too long ago.

I feel calmer now that I've figured that out. I guess I shouldn't be so quick to judge people. But I wish there were more people here who really cared about Sarah, who didn't just know her by her port-wine stain. I wish there were more people who missed her the way I do.

And then I listen to some of the other kids talking, hear the stories they tell. They remember Sarah standing up to bullies, giving half her sandwich to a girl who'd forgotten her lunch, picking up an essay that someone dropped in a crowded hall and handing it back to them. They remember a smile and a kind word on a day they felt miserable, money loaned and never asked for back, a comic given to a girl whose parents had split up. She touched a lot of lives through small kindnesses and brave actions, over and over again, even with people who ignored her or treated her like dirt. A lot of people are feeling her absence. I wish I could tell her that. I hope she knows.

SARAH

IT'S BEEN EIGHT DAYS since Brian's been here. Two days without food. And one without water. I worry that I misjudged him. Worry that he really is leaving me here to die — the slow, torturous death of starvation or dehydration. Worry that this is what he planned all along.

I think of all the times I said, "I'm starving!" or "I'm dying of thirst," and I cringe. If I ever get out of here, I'll never say that again.

I struggle to breathe evenly, to keep myself from crying, from discharging some of my body's precious water. I feel the cold so much more keenly without food in me. I force myself to walk to keep warm. It must have been Brian the other day, coming to check on me. I guess he can't face killing me himself. He's waiting for nature to do it.

"Well, I'm not dead yet, you bastard!" I yell.

I find myself thinking of my favorite comic books at the

strangest times. Like when I'm going on the bucket, or when I'm trying not to cry. Even without being able to read them again, they are a comfort and an escape. If I ever get out of here, I want to write a comic book like that. A comic book people remember. One that moves people, that gives them hope.

I've started to mark the days with balls of foil I've made from the seal off the peanut butter jar — one ball for each day. It helps me feel like I have some control, and it's something to do when I need a rest from the boards. I wonder what I'll mark time with when I run out of foil. I guess I can start on the cracker box. I laugh, my voice hoarse and strange in the quiet, my throat like sandpaper. It's sore, like when I was eight and had strep throat. Mom kept bringing me juice, tea with honey, cough drops, but nothing helped, not until Dad came home and did a puppet show for me.

I have a sudden image of them hunched over the kitchen table, talking to a police officer, their faces pale and drawn. I wish I could speak to them one last time, tell them how much I love them. Dad is easy to love — he's so encouraging and supportive. Mom is harder, with her always trying to force me not to care about my cheek — but I do love her. I wish I'd told her more.

I've got to stop thinking like that. I dig my nails into the soft flesh between my thumb and forefinger. I will tell them when I get back home. I wish I were there now, laughing at Dad's corny jokes, chatting with Mom while we do the dishes, feeling surrounded by their love.

I was so sure I'd be out of here by now, so sure I was smarter than Brian. But I'm not stronger than wood and nails. I can feel myself collapsing inside, wanting him to come just for the food and water he'll bring.

I hear the crunch of tires on gravel, the slam of a car door, then metal scraping against metal, and a thud as the bar is pushed aside. I scramble to my feet and press myself against the wall near the door, waiting.

The door opens, bringing cool air and the scent of salt-laden, greasy french fries, a juicy hamburger, and rich hot chocolate.

Saliva fills my mouth so fast I can hardly swallow. I want that food so badly. It's all I can smell as Brian steps inside, all I can think about. The door slams shut, and like that, my chance of escape is gone.

I can feel Brian's gaze on me, and I know he's watching, waiting for me to react. To beg.

Well, I'm not going to. I stand still, my legs shaky, my head too light.

Brian stands so close to me that I can feel his body heat. The smell of those french fries is overpowering. I keep swallowing my own saliva.

"You hungry, Sarah?" Brian asks, almost pleasantly.

Damn it, he knows I am. He has to know that he didn't leave me enough food. "Yes," I say hoarsely.

"I thought you might be." I hear his skin brush against cardboard, smell the wonderful greasy potatoes, hear him chomp loudly, then swallow. "Well, here's what I'm going to do. You admit that you've been manipulating everyone — your family, your friends — into thinking poor little you needs extra attention because of that mark on your cheek, and I'll give you some fries. Heck, I'll give you the whole container if I believe you mean it."

I want those fries so badly I can already taste them. But the old shame flushes through me, pushing the heat up from my chest to my face. Mikey, coming up behind me, chanting, "Purple face, purple face!" Me bursting into tears. Old Mrs. Barton, standing at the front of the first grade classroom, shaking her finger at me: "Sarah Meadows, don't think I'm going to give you special treatment. You stop that crying right now, or you can stand up here and let the whole class look at you." Me, standing with my back to the whiteboard, the chemical stink of markers clogging my nose, Mrs. Barton forcing my head up with the end of her yardstick, kids' laughter ringing through the room, and through my nightmares for years afterward.

I take a deep, shaky breath. "When I can fly like Superman."

Brian laughs — a short, hard bark. "You're spunky. But you sure don't have much sense. I know you're hungry; you've got to be. Admit the truth and you can have this entire meal. Even the hot chocolate."

I want that hot chocolate so fiercely I can hardly think. My stomach is eating itself, pain pulling it inward. I know I can't keep going without food. But he's trying to fuck with my head. If I give in to him, what will he do to me next? "I'm just as strong as anyone else, maybe even stronger because of the way people treat me. And I've never pretended otherwise."

Brian clucks his tongue. "Sorry to hear that. It's bye-bye fries." He walks a few steps away, and the door grates open, then slams shut. The stairs vibrate. I can feel the emptiness of the room, the stillness, like he's shut me inside a coffin.

For a few seconds I can't believe he gave up so fast. Can't believe he really took the fries with him, the only food I've smelled in days. Can't believe I let him go. I should have charged the door, but I wouldn't have made it, anyway, not weak like this.

"No, wait!" I cry, smacking the door with my palms. "Wait, I'll say it!"

But there's only silence.

I slide down the door, too faint to stand. I almost had french fries. Hot chocolate. What's wrong with me? My survival is more important than the truth.

Tears soak the blindfold. I feel helplessly weak and stupid. I don't know what is right anymore. I cry until my eyes hurt, until I can't bear to cry anymore.

I lean my head back wearily. What if I die here, all because I wouldn't regurgitate some stupid words? I can't afford to fight him too hard, not while he's holding my life in his hands.

Heavy footsteps sound on the stairs.

I push myself up off the floor and away from the door.

"Have you rethought things, Sarah?" Brian asks as he comes in.

"I made people think I was a victim so they would take care of me and give me attention," I say.

"Why?" Brian asks cheerfully.

Why? For a moment I can't remember. "My cheek," I say.

"Very good, Sarah." Brian touches my head. "I'm afraid I got bored waiting for you to change your mind. I finished everything off."

The tears start again. I hate my weakness.

"Except for —" There's a rattle inside cardboard. "Two lone fries. Think you'd like them?"

"Yes!" I say hoarsely.

"What? I couldn't hear you."

"Yes, please, could I have the fries?" I say, worried that he's going to take them away again.

"Here you are," Brian says gently, grasping my hand and turning it palm upward. He shakes the two fries into my hand. "You see how easy it is when you just cooperate?"

I barely hear him. I ram the limp, cold fries into my mouth, feel their once-crisp edges, their soft potato insides, the grease and salt almost giving me a high. Before I can control myself, I swallow, and they're gone. Gone, and I am desperate for more.

"Glad you've come to your senses," Brian says. "Nobody's out there looking for you, you know."

"Yes, they are!"

"Nope. People think you ran away. A troubled, selfish girl, upset about not getting the treatments she was promised, treatments she was relying on to make her life better."

I can't catch my breath. "You're lying!"

But even if he isn't, the police look for runaways, don't they? I've got to keep him from messing with my head.

"Why would I lie about that? It's all going as it should. Everyone's always seen you as sullen, angry, and withdrawn. Bullied at school, insecure, unhappy at home — a high risk as a runaway. Even your best friend sees you that way."

"She does not!"

"Sure she does. Why else do you think she hangs out with you? She feels sorry for you."

"You don't know anything about it!" But maybe he does. Maybe I've been lying to myself this whole time. I thought Charlene and I became friends because we both know what it's like to be outsiders. But maybe I was a pity friend.

No — that can't be right. My legs won't stop trembling.

Brian touches my stained cheek.

I swat his hand away and try to bite him before I even think about it.

"Don't be like that. You should be thanking me. I'm giving your parents a blessing. No more guilt every time they think of you — just a weight off their shoulders, a relief greater than any they've known since the day you were born."

He's obsessed with my port-wine stain. It does something to him — unleashes the darkness inside him.

I rub my cheek. "Why do I have to have this blindfold on? Is there something you don't want me to see?"

"I thought you were smart. You figure it out."

Something must fuel his obsession. But he looks so perfect. "You must have a port-wine stain, too — one you can hide. Maybe on your leg or your chest?"

Brian slams me up against the wall. "Don't try to make me like you! We're nothing alike. *Nothing!*"

I'm right. I know I am. When something that's a part of you causes you so much pain — pain others inflict — you obsess about it. I know. "It's nothing to be ashamed of. Whatever anybody told you —"

"Will you shut up?" His lips press hard against mine, sucking away my air.

I taste salty fries, hamburger, and onions. I am grossed out, yet so fiercely hungry, I want to suck down any particles left.

His lips keep working against mine, like he's trying to swallow me. I punch him, but he doesn't seem to notice. He keeps stroking my cheek.

I shudder. This is what it's about. This is what it's been about all along. I know it deep in my gut.

Brian brushes his knuckles against my cheek almost roughly, and then he is pushing me to the uneven floor, the wood creaking beneath us.

No! I fight him, but I am so weak that my punches are like a fly against his back. I almost don't care. I just want it to be over.

"That's good, Judy," Brian whispers in my ear, his unshaven cheek pricking my skin. "It's so good."

Coldness runs through me. "It's Sarah," I say, though I don't know why I tell him.

"Sarah," Brian says, and pushes my hair from my face. "That's what I said."

But I know he's called me by a dead girl's name. I jerk beneath his hands.

He moves against me, and I think I should feel something, but I feel nothing, not even pain, just a dull waiting for this to be over, for the monotony of my life to start up again. Because he means to keep me alive, at least for a while longer, or he wouldn't have brought me food.

I drift away from my body, from the room. Dad and Mom

will look for me. I know they will. And Charlene will, too. Maybe even Nick. I feel a small rush of warmth.

I keep my mind on Nick, draw him closer to me, see his soulful eyes, his soft face, the way he looks at me as if he knows my heart and likes what he sees. I make him more real than this room, than the man on top of me. I make Nick so vivid that we must be connecting somehow. I'm sure he can hear me, if only I can think loudly enough at him, the way Professor X can.

Nick, who loves comics as much as I do, who believes in good and evil, who knows what it's like not to belong. Who wants to believe in superpowers as much as I do. If anyone could connect with me telepathically and understand what is happening, it would be him.

Pain rips through me, and Nick's face starts to fade. But I won't let him go.

I visualize Brian as I saw him last, his handsome face distorted, and I imagine sending it to Nick in bursts. *Find me, Nick. Save me.*

NICK
DAY 10, 7:30 P.M.

NO ONE'S SEEN HER. I don't know how anyone can just vanish, but it happens. It happens way too often, and it's driving me insane. I wish superpowers were real, wish I could hear her call for help the way Superman always hears Lois.

I stuff another cookie in my mouth, crumbs falling onto my keyboard. I can barely taste the sweetness, don't even like it, but still I eat. I eat to numb the feelings inside me. The dread. The fear. The pain. Without even noticing, I've gone through half the package of cookies. I push the box aside, feeling queasy.

She must be so afraid, my Sarah. So alone. I need her found and brought back home. I've imagined swooping in like Superman to save her, but I really don't care who does it or how it happens; I just want her back. Back with her family, back with me at school, giving me little snippets of her time. She's not dead. I know Old Fart-a-Lot thinks she is. Even the cops do. But I don't.

If she comes back, I'm not going to hide anymore. I'm going to show her how I feel.

I break out my pencils and markers, my comic paper, and I draw Sarah the way I see her — brave and fierce. But it's not enough somehow. I stare off into space, letting my mind wander — and then I know how to show her the way I see her. The way she really is. I draw her as Diamond, fighting the bad guys, stopping abductions and rapes and things most comics never address. It's just me and Sarah/Diamond against the world — and we win. We win every single time.

SARAH

I DON'T KNOW HOW long it's been this time. Even with the foil balls, it's hard to keep track. But he's back. I just heard his car door slam. I tense, waiting.

The stairs shake, then the door scrapes open. I charge toward the cold air, determined to make it. Brian throws me backwards. I hit the floor hard, my teeth jarring. I scramble up again, panting, but the door has already grated shut.

"When are you going to learn that this is your home?" Brian asks calmly, as if what he's saying is reasonable.

I hear a thump as he sets something down.

"Well?" he says.

"My home is with my parents."

"Not that again," Brian says, and sighs heavily.

I feel him watching me.

"And what are those stupid foil balls for?"

My tongue sticks to the roof of my mouth.

"Well?"

Do I admit the truth to him or not? "They're for counting the days."

He snorts. "What difference will that make?"

None. He's right; it won't get me out of here.

I shrug and take a step back, my jeans chafing. Can he smell my period blood? Can he see it? My body has betrayed me, bleeding when I can't stop its flow. When I can't even do the most basic thing to keep myself clean, to have some sort of dignity.

I clench my hands. "I . . . I need something."

"You do, do you?" Brian says slowly. "What do you want?"

I swallow and try to keep the shame out of my voice. "Women's things. You know. For that time of the month."

"Ah," Brian says. "Of course. And what are you going to do for it? You haven't showed me that you've learned anything."

A blaze of heat ignites in my chest. I don't want to dance to his tune. But I have to if I want to stop the bleeding. "I manipulate people."

"That's the lesson all right, but I don't hear you believing it," Brian says, his voice closer than it was a moment ago.

I try to add more feeling. "I manipulated my parents."

He steps even closer. "Yes, you did. And you acted like a victim, trying to get people to take care of you. You know that, don't you?"

"Yes," I hear myself saying.

"Hmm. I think you're beginning to learn." He strokes my cheek. "Very well. You've earned a reward."

Dare I ask him for one more thing while he's in such a good mood? I run my tongue over my dry lips. "Thanks. And could I please also have some toilet paper?"

"You're really pushing it, aren't you?" Brian says, his voice hard. Then he sighs, "I suppose you've earned it."

I hear him leave. I find my way to the door, but he's locked it again. He's never forgotten yet. I keep hoping he will.

Brian knocks me back when he reenters, then thrusts something soft into my hands.

I feel it with my fingers. "What—?"

"Rags," Brian says pleasantly. "That's what you've earned."

"Thank you," I choke out, trying to sound grateful so he won't take them away.

"And this." He pushes a soft, round roll into my hands.

Toilet paper. Gratefulness makes me weep.

"You're really beginning to stink."

My body burns. "If you give me soap, some deoderant . . ."

"You won't be here long enough to bother."

He pushes me to the floor, his hands undoing my jeans. I leave my body faster this time.

SARAH

I KNOW I SHOULD be grateful. I've slept and woken many times, and I'm still not dead. I have food again — more crackers, peanut butter, and bananas. And three jugs of water. But I am so sick of the thick, nutty taste of peanut butter, the sweet pulpiness of bananas, and the salty dryness of crackers that I have to force them down. I dream of those two french fries. I wake up smelling them, and when I realize it's just peanut butter, it's hard not to cry. And I long to smell fresh air, to see the faces of the people I love, to be able to walk about freely.

Wind howls through the hole in the door, raging and wailing, blowing in bits of snow that melt on my skin. I shiver and wrap the thermal blanket tighter around me, then crawl back to my corner under the down comforter. I hope the snow doesn't bury my prison. I need a way to get out. And as much as I hate to admit it, I need a way for Brian to get in.

He's been coming by more often. I don't know if that's a good thing or a bad thing. Except that he brings food and water, and I'm still alive.

But his words keep circling through my head, telling me that I act like a victim. As much as I don't want to, I keep remembering times that prove him right, like that time I tried to get a job.

The little fruit market in our neighborhood had a hand-lettered sign in the grimy window: PART-TIME HELP NEEDED. APPLY WITHIN. No one had ever hired me to do anything, not even babysit. But I wanted to start saving for my treatments.

So I walked into the shop, steeling myself as the jangling bell announced me. The warm air smelled like a mixture of ripening fruit and mustiness. I kept my head tilted so my hair covered my cheek. A woman with streaks of gray in her thick black hair shuffled up to the counter. Her wrinkled face looked weary. She was definitely a five. Nothing beautiful about her, but nothing ugly, either. Just a regular person that most people didn't even notice. How I wanted that.

"Yes, yes, can I help you?" The woman looked at me closer, then leaned over the chipped counter to get a better look. "What happen to your face?"

What happened to your manners? I wanted to snap, but I sucked the words back.

"What happen?" the woman said again, her voice loud and insistent. The other customers turned to look.

My face grew warm. "Nothing happened," I mumbled. "I was born like this."

"Eh?" the woman said, cocking her ear toward me.

The other customers busied themselves among the bins of fruit, but I could feel them taking peeks at me. I wanted to flatten inward until there was nothing left for anyone to stare at. But if I could pay for the treatments, maybe Mom would let me have them, and then I wouldn't have to go through this anymore. I spoke loudly enough so they could all hear me. "It's a port-wine stain; I was born with it."

"Ah." The woman nodded, then looked away, like she was embarrassed by me now.

I took another breath. "I wanted to apply for the part-time job?"

The woman shook her head. "No, no. No job."

"No job?" I clenched my hands together. "But the sign in the window says—"

"No job right now. You come back later, okay? Later." She nodded and turned away.

I stood there, confused. Did she mean there were no jobs for me because of my face? Or did she mean to come back later that day, when someone else would be there?

Another customer looked at me, curiosity and sympathy in her eyes. I rushed out of the store, and I never went back. Never tried anywhere else, either. Maybe I did act like a victim.

No. I wanted to be treated with respect, and I didn't get it there. Okay, maybe I tried to shield myself from more rejection. But who doesn't do that? That's not being a victim. I've got to keep myself from being sucked into Brian's lies. Nothing he says to me is true.

I get up, feel my way over to the window, and tug on the boards again.

NICK
DAY 27, 5:30 P.M.

I HOPE SARAH'S STILL alive. I pray that she is. But it's getting harder to believe that she might be. It's been almost a month since she went missing.

I square my shoulders and walk into the police station, where I get the clerk to call the detective down.

"You again," the detective says, looking at me sourly. I've come by once a week since Sarah disappeared. You'd think he'd expect me by now.

"Don't want me to drop by? Then find Sarah!"

The detective shakes his head wearily. "It's not like we haven't been trying. Your coming here, hassling me like this — it only eats up valuable working time."

"Right. Like you were searching for her when the desk clerk phoned you."

"Hey — I've got twenty-five other cases I have to deal with on top of hers. And all are just as important."

"Just as important as a missing girl?" I say.

"You'd be surprised. Look, kid — you can't keep coming by here, asking for me. I want to get Sarah Meadows back, too. But this isn't the way to do it." He takes a step toward the door, holding out his hand to usher me out.

"Then what is?" I say, not moving.

The detective shrugs. "If I knew, we'd be doing it. We're already doing everything we can."

Code words for "we've almost given up."

"Just — don't stop looking. Sarah's a good person. Brave, smart, and kind. She doesn't deserve this."

"None of them do, son," the detective says sadly.

I leave before I yell at him. That won't get me anywhere. I can't believe how easily a missing person gets pushed aside after barely a month. A life has to be worth more than that. Sarah is worth more than that. I rip open a bag of chips and stuff a handful in my mouth. Anger churns through my gut.

I head toward the Meadowses' house. I go over as often as I can. They've become a second family to me. We find comfort in one another's grief, and in our hope. In a world that doesn't seem to care, that doesn't support our belief that Sarah is still alive, we buoy one another up. The reporters have stopped calling. The only ones who talk about Sarah now are the gossip rags, and even they don't have much to say, and nothing hopeful. But as long as they keep Sarah in people's minds, I guess it's a good thing. I throw my empty chip bag in the trash and dust off my hands and face.

Brian is leaving just as I come in. We nod at each other, our faces tight with worry. "Distract her, will you?" he whispers. "She wouldn't let me."

"I'll try," I whisper back. I close the door behind him.

Mrs. Meadows is sitting at the kitchen table, printing off photo after photo of Sarah. She painstakingly places them in an album while tears stream down her cheeks.

I sit down tentatively at the table with her. "Wow, that's a lot of photos," I say.

Mrs. Meadows looks up at me, scissors in one hand, photo that she's been trimming in the other. "I never took the time to go through all our photos; I was always too busy. Sure, I kept an album, and one for Sarah, too — but there are so many other photos that should be in them. So many sweet images." She's crying harder now.

"Here, let me help you," I say, and gently take the scissors from her shaking hand. I think she needs someone else to remember and love Sarah along with her more than she needs to be distracted. I finish trimming the photo of six-year-old Sarah lying in a hammock reading a comic. "Tell me about this one," I say.

Mrs. Meadows's face lights up as she tells me about what Sarah was like as a kid, and I soak up every word.

Later, walking home, I feel closer to Sarah, even though it hurts, too. I wish Charlene would come with me to the Meadowses' — her pain and guilt is eating her like cancer — but she can't handle their grief. She says it's so heavy and dark at the Meadowses' that it's like being underground. It's funny that she can't feel the hope there. It's what helps me get through.

I worry about Charlene. I know she's flunking classes, spacing out like I do, but she's also got her crap of a dad going at her, tearing her down. And her mom, while nice, doesn't seem to understand. At least my dad kind of gets it — we both went through something like this when Mom died. Only Sarah's not dead. I won't give up believing she's still out there. And in a way that makes it harder. The grief just keeps dragging on and on; we don't know when or if she'll ever be found. But I have to believe she will be. Alive.

I try to explain to my dad why I'm spending so much time with the Meadowses. He doesn't think it's healthy, and we've had a few yelling matches, but he always comes around. His mom left him when he was little, and he spent most of his life looking for her. So I guess he gets it. I just wish Charlene's parents did.

She's spending more and more time with Gemma. People are talking about them, but I don't think she cares, maybe for the first time in her life. Sometimes she looks almost happy with Gemma. I know I should be glad for her, but I envy her that. I don't know how to be happy without Sarah. And maybe I don't want to be.

SARAH

I WONDER IF THEY'VE forgotten me. If they've all gotten on with their lives. Not Dad and Mom — I know they must be missing me the way I'm missing them. But Charlene, Nick — do they even think of me anymore? Do they take a moment from the drama in their lives to wonder where I am?

It's been thirty-five days that I've been gone — at least, as far as I can figure. I make a new ball whenever I get up after a long sleep, and I count them whenever I'm too tired or depressed to do anything else. I've got to stop feeling sorry for myself. Stop feeling so lost. But I do feel lost. And forgotten.

Every day I grow more desperate, more afraid that this will be the day he gets tired of me, the day when I feel his knife slice through my flesh — but so far it hasn't happened. So I try to keep hoping I'll get out of here alive. And I imagine what it'll be like if I do. How I'll be different.

If I ever get out of here, I'll stop judging people by how they look. It's all a lie, anyway. Take Brian — he looks gorgeous, but he's the ugliest person I've ever met. *He* should be rated a minus five, not me. I keep wondering how I missed seeing his cruelty. Every time I think about it, I remember those twinges of uneasiness that I pushed away. The instincts I ignored. I swear if I ever get out of here, I'll never ignore my gut again.

If I ever get out of here, I'm going to give Nick a chance. Who cares what other people think? It's my life, for however long I've got. If I don't do what feels right to me, what I need and want to do, then am I really living?

If I ever get out of here, I won't hide my face anymore. I swear it. If anyone should hide his face, it's Brian. I practice tucking my hair behind my ears and holding my head up higher.

I'm afraid I'll forget these promises to myself if I ever get back to the real world. Afraid I'll lose my courage and let what's important get buried by all the tiny stresses and worries of everyday life, things that seem so important at the time, but sure aren't now. So I make the promises into a comic, and I tell the story over and over to myself. Diamond always hid her scarred arm, wounds her father cut into her when she was a child, but after she faces a monster who looks so sweet that he draws his victims to him, Diamond knows what she has to do. She rips the sleeve off her costume, baring her jagged scars, and keeps rescuing people. When some people in the crowd act shocked or repulsed, Diamond calmly tells them her scars are part of her past, part of what made her who she is. And then when Diamond sees the boy she loves in the crowd, she asks him out, right there in front of everyone. Even though some people in the crowd laugh, Diamond feels stronger than ever. That's what I want to be — emotionally stronger. Able to do what feels right to me, even if no one else understands.

I drag myself up off the floor and walk the circuit of the room once, twice, three times. I have to force myself to; it's getting harder to care. But I've got to keep myself warm, and fit enough to escape. Ready for the moment when my chance comes.

I go to the boards on the window, find the one I always work on, and yank at it. Its rough surface nips at my skin like a piranha, but I grip the board harder and yank again. It may be hopeless, but I can't stop trying. I can't bear to just sit here. So I work the board, my fingertips getting raw, and I tell myself another story. A story of escape.

NICK
DAY 43, 6:30 P.M.

I MISS SARAH EVERY day. It's not getting any easier. No, that's a lie — sometimes I find myself laughing at a joke, or looking up at the bright blue sky and finding it beautiful. But afterward I always wish that Sarah were here sharing it with me, and then I'm back to sad again. Sad and determined. I'm not giving up on her — but it feels like I am.

I can't believe that Dad dragged me to the mall to get new jeans. I don't care that my old ones have holes in them. But it was easier to go with him than to put up a fight, and besides, he looked lonely. I haven't seen much of him, what with all the time I spend at the Meadowses'.

When I saw Charlene and Gemma together in the food court, I couldn't look away. Charlene was crying, but then Gemma reached out and took her hand, all tender-like, and a little later they were laughing.

I wanted to grab hold of the railings and scream down at

them. I was surprised by how furious I felt. And then I realized I was angry because they have what I want.

I want to reach for Sarah's hand and feel her startle, all surprised. She'll look at me with big eyes, and then see how much I love her, and then pretty soon the two of us will be laughing, just for the joy of being together. I want that so much, my chest hurts.

I don't know what to do with all my emotion. I usually try to eat it away, but it's not working. So lately I've been putting it into my art. Into the comics I draw for Sarah. I draw her defiant and strong, the way she was when she protected Googly Eyes from those boys. I draw her bold and sure, the way she was when she stood up for Madison. I keep drawing her until my fingers are numb, hoping to draw her back into my life.

Every panel, every pencil stroke, is for her. I draw in black-and-white; there's no color in my life. But if she gets home — *when* she gets home — the color will come back.

I know some of the guys online think I'm lame, mooning over a girl who might never come home, a girl who may never love me back. But I think that's because they've never felt real love. Because if they had, they'd be crying with me. Not that I cry. Okay, I do. But so what? I'm human. I hurt. I love. I hope. I still effing hope.

Maybe I am crazy, holding on to hope. But at least I'm not alone in it. Mr. and Mrs. Meadows hope just as hard as I do.

Even Brian has hope. Today he told Mrs. Meadows, "I can't even pretend to know how you feel, but I think everything will be okay in the long run."

Mrs. Meadows burst into tears, and Brian pulled her to him, hugging her. "Remember, I'm here for you, anytime you need me," he murmured, patting her back while Mr. Meadows and I watched, our own eyes tearing up.

You've got so many people who care about you, Sarah. So come home.

SARAH

I AM TIRED OF my if-I-ever-get-out-of-here daydreams. I'm even tired of creating comics — never being able to write them down, just composing snatches in my head, forgetting bits, and starting all over again. The stories I tell myself aren't enough anymore. I'm just so tired. I want an end to this. I want to be home. And when my despair is strong, like it is now, I think maybe I'd rather not be here at all if I can't go back. If I have to keep living this hell that's not quite a life. I'm tired of hoping, of trying so hard and never succeeding.

I tell myself I need to get up and work on the board again, but I just sit here, hopelessness like lead in my bones, weighing me down. What's the point of trying when I know I'll never escape? It's been more than a month, and I haven't managed to get even one board off. But Diamond would never give up. Neither would my mom and dad. I have to keep hoping.

Outside this room, time is passing without me. It's getting

warmer, turning into spring. I can tell by the air blowing through the hole; it doesn't have the same cold bite. I'm missing it all. I long to feel the sun on my skin, to press my fingers into the dirt and smell its richness, to look up at the bright blue of the sky and see the birds flying across. I long to be outside, free, the way I always was, without even being aware of it. If I ever get out of here, I swear I will notice things like that. I will appreciate them.

Dad and Mom must still be looking for me. They won't have given up — even if they believe I've run away, like Brian said they do. Despair washes through me so strongly that I don't want to live. But I can't let myself go there. So I picture their faces in my mind and try to hear their voices.

Charlene and Nick must be gearing up for spring break. I wonder if they've forgotten me already. Or if they think of me fondly sometimes, before they go back to their own lives.

The days are so long, the nights even longer. Without my sight, I have only temperature changes and my body's rhythms to give me a sense of passing time, and the foil balls I use to mark it with. The monotony, the days and days of no contact with anyone, makes me want to scream just to hear another human voice. I talk aloud to myself. If I didn't, I think I'd go crazy. I'm not sure I haven't gone a little crazy already. I never understood that expression that none of us is an island, but I get it now. I need to hear someone's voice, need to feel someone touch my skin so badly that I start imagining it, hallucinating it, until it's almost real.

I can almost hear Mom reading me *Guess How Much I Love You*, but her voice and the words fade when I try to hold on to them. Tears well up behind my eyelids. I must have made her read me that book a thousand times when I was little. So why can't I remember better? And what does that say about me, that I needed to hear it so often? That I didn't believe she really loved me? Maybe Brian is right. Maybe I was picking something up from her. From her and Dad both.

But I think of the way Mom would smooth my hair back from my face, her touch so gentle, and the way Dad would sit beside me for hours, the two of us reading comics, playing board games, watching old movies, and I know that they love me.

As often as I imagine them, it's getting hard to remember exactly what they sound like, the way Mom's voice rises when she laughs, and Dad's gets deeper. Brian's voice is the one that fills my mind, reverberating inside me until it is all I can hear.

I wonder if they're thinking about me right now, if they can feel me thinking about them — if Mom turns around, startled, putting her hand to her cheek to try to catch my touch, if Dad leans forward in his chair, trying to hear my voice. I want that connection to be there. I don't want them to give up on me, the way Brian says they have.

His lies find their way inside my skull, building up like sediment.

"Your parents have stopped looking for you. They're spending all their time trying to save your dad's company. Money is more important to them. It always is."

"Charlene's forgotten all about you — and she found herself a girlfriend; can you believe it? Gemma, I think her name is."

"Your parents aren't looking for you, because they're the ones who wanted to get rid of you. They paid me to take you."

I don't believe him, not really. But I've heard his lies so many times, they almost sound normal to me, like the sound of my own heartbeat.

I know they're out there looking for me — Dad craning his head as he drives, looking at every girl my height, my weight, stopping at every gas station to ask about me; Mom walking the sidewalks, carrying flyers that she shoves at every passerby.

They won't give up on me. They love me too much for that.

But a part of me isn't sure that's true.

I clench my fists, scabs breaking open. I can't let Brian's lies become my reality. I have to believe I'll get out of here, and that Mom and Dad will be glad when I'm back.

The first thing I want when I get home is food. Real food, food that fills me up on the inside. My stomach growls, tight with hunger, but I can't let myself eat tomorrow's rations. Can't let myself eat as much as I want or need. I have to be smart.

Time seems endless when Brian isn't here, but it's better than when he's with me. He checks the buckles on my blindfold every visit, tightens the straps when they get loose. And I can feel him watch me when I sit on the bucket. I know he can hear every tinkle, every plop I make, must smell the horrible stink, and so I try to hold it in when he is here. It becomes a test of wills between us, but eventually my body always betrays me. My body betrays me, too, in being hungry when he offers me food, in being thirsty when he brings me water. In making me need him to survive. But nothing can make me like him.

I've stopped swatting his hand away from my cheek, stopped shaking my hair out over my port-wine stain. He'll just force me to expose my cheek again. There's something about my trying to hide, something about my shame that goads him on. And he's already seen my cheek, touched it more than anyone ever has except my parents. So now I keep my cheek bare, and let him touch it when he wants. I think it unnerves him.

The last time I thrust my bared cheek forward, I felt him hesitate, heard him draw in his breath as if it scared him. I hope it did.

Wheels crunch along gravel. A car door slams. His feet shake the steps, and then the door grates open. Cool air pushes at my face.

I have to remember not to fight back. He goes easier on me when I give in.

The door thuds shut. Footsteps come toward me. I stand still, my head held high, trying to keep from trembling.

"You're not going to rush me? I'm shocked," Brian says.

I shrug. "It never works."

"You got that right."

The floorboards groan, and the sharp, piney scent of his cologne fills the room. "You're not even going to beg me to let you go? You're slipping."

"I thought that's what you wanted. For me to accept my place."

"True . . ."

But he doesn't sound happy. Maybe he enjoys the fight. Maybe that's what's keeping me alive, even though he says he wants me to comply. "You can't keep me here. They're going to find me!"

"You know that isn't true." He strokes my cheek gently, and I let him. "Why do you keep lying to yourself?"

"Why do you?" I shoot back. "They're going to catch you. When I get out of here, everyone will know what you did. My dad will come after you. They all will."

Brian makes a clucking sound with his tongue. "You're dreaming. But let's say, for argument's sake, that you did manage to escape. Then I would have to kill your parents. It would be your fault they died. Do you really want to make that happen? I've told you—they're better off without you. Without the burden you create for them."

He's crazy, absolutely crazy—but I believe him. He will kill my parents if I escape. How can I ever try to leave now?

But I can't stay. I will die. There's got to be a way that I can escape and still warn them in time. Or maybe he's just bluffing.

"Ah. I can see by your expression that you've been trying to free yourself. I knew you were stronger than those other girls, even if your actions are misguided. Just remember: if you get out, your family dies."

I turn my head away from his voice, trying to keep my face impassive. I can't let him see my fear. He's too insidious, twisting his logic to fit my reactions.

Brian's footsteps creak across the floor as he paces the room. I wait, praying he won't see my attempts to loosen the board.

He comes to stand in front of me again, his cologne so thick in the air, I cough.

"Whatever you've been doing, it's going to stop. You need to accept your fate. This is where you belong."

I shake my head no.

"Yes." Brian grips my cheeks between his fingers and thumb, squeezng hard, then lets me go. "Your parents gave up on you the day you were born. You don't have anyone in the world who loves you — except me."

"My parents love me." I say it quietly, but not quietly enough.

"Will you stop your nattering? I swear, I thought you were smarter than this. They feel guilty about your face. Guilt isn't love."

Liar! I pinch my lips together to hold in the words.

"If they really loved you, they'd be spending all their time looking for you, but they're not. They're just trying to save your dad's business. It's doing much better now that you're not around to worry them."

"That doesn't even make sense. It wasn't in trouble until the day you took me." *Was it?*

"*You* made your dad's business fail when you asked for those laser treatments," he says.

Something inside me shifts. "You're lying!" My voice shakes. "You're just trying to suck me into your crazy world!"

"Don't be silly. Think about it — why haven't they tried harder to find you? Because they could have if they really wanted to. It's all there in front of them."

"They *are* looking for me," I say, though I'm no longer sure if that's true.

"Sarah, Sarah." Brian sighs heavily. "Why can't you make this easy on yourself? Learn what you have to learn. Stop resisting me. I can see I'll have to teach you another lesson. Your dad's business started failing the day he made the appointment for your laser treatments. He was distracted by you and your mother fighting, so he wasn't watching things closely. It was all too easy to take advantage of him."

My heart clenches. "*You're* the one who stole from him!"

"Misappropriated his funds." I can hear Brian smile. "And that was just the beginning. I can make their lives hell if you don't learn what you have to learn."

His fingers dig into my arm. Anger rises like heat off his skin.

I never should have argued with him. I can't bear the thought of him hurting Dad and Mom even more.

He yanks at my jeans, jerking at the fabric.

I swallow. I know what he wants to hear. I hope he believes me. "I guess they have felt guilty about my face."

"Of course they have."

He thrusts me back against the wall, his hands rough on my skin.

I keep talking, my tongue thick. "I know it's hard on them. I've seen their pain when people are mean to me."

"Exactly." His hands are almost gentle now.

Brian's sharp cologne slices through my body odor, his bristly lips scratch my skin, and I feel myself slip away from my body to float up above it all. I watch from the ceiling as if I can astral travel like Raven, the Teen Titan. I wish I had her teleportation power instead, to vanish myself out of here.

"You're so beautiful," Brian whispers.

I hear Mom's voice echoing Brian's, and I want to shut them out, but their voices go on and on, following the rhythm of my breath, until they drown out the sound of Brian moving against me.

NICK
DAY 67, 2:00 A.M.

I WISH I COULD track Sarah down by her scent the way Wolverine could and bring her home safe. I scowl into the semidarkness of my bedroom, the glow from my laptop like a night-light. I know it's stupid to think like that. Life is not a comic book; not even close. If it were, Sarah would be home right now. Instead, she's still out there somewhere, scared and hurting.

I'm dog tired, but to sleep feels like I'm betraying her, leaving her all alone. So I haunt the website, create new comics, do anything to connect to her. Sometimes I feel like I'm the only one who still cares. Me and the Meadowses and Brian.

Brian dropped by again today, bringing muffins and coffee. Mrs. Meadows just picked at them.

"You don't have to keep doing this," she said. "You've got a job as long as you want it, as long as we can afford it. Thomas said you're brilliant at what you do."

Brian smiled, but he looked sad, somehow. "That's not why I'm here. I want to make things easier for you, Ellen. You seem to be in such pain all the time."

"I just — I miss her," Mrs. Meadows said, covering her mouth with a shaking hand. "I miss her, and I worry about her."

"I know you do." Brian patted her hand. Then he jerked his chin at me. "Buck up, Nick. Try to help Ellen, here."

"Oh, he does!" Mrs. Meadows said quickly.

For a moment I wanted to hit him, but I know he was saying it only because I looked as down as Mrs. Meadows did.

But Charlene doesn't look down, not anymore. I saw her and Gemma in the Java Cup on my way home. Charlene was holding Gemma's hand across the table, staring into her eyes like she was love struck. It made me want to smash something. Why is it that Charlene gets happiness while Sarah and I don't?

But I know why. I never made my move. And there were so many times I could have. Like that time in the comic shop when Sarah had a rant. She flung down the comic she'd been reading like it disgusted her.

Geordie, the clerk, glared at her. "Lucky you already bought that copy."

"Yeah, well, you can take it off my pull file. I can't stand it anymore," Sarah said, her eyes all fiery.

"Stand what?" Geordie asked, clicking away at his computer.

"How . . . *weak* she is. ClawBright should be as strong as Superman or the Hulk—but no, she's got half the power and is so messed up she needs a male's hero guidance to figure anything out."

I never thought of ClawBright like that before. But she was right.

"And why does she always have to be dressed like a hooker? And with such big . . . big . . ."

"Boobs?" Geordie said, scratching his belly. "I like them."

"You would."

I could see other customers listening. Some even stopped pulling comics to watch.

"I know what you mean," I said shyly. "It's like her superpower is her looks. She's a pin-up for guys to drool over. Not a serious character like Batwoman."

"Exactly!" Sarah said, turning to me gratefully. She looked surprised when she recognized me, and yet I thought I saw a brief flash of admiration or maybe just respect, and then it was gone.

"Hey—they're just catering to the clientele," Geordie said. "Most of the buyers are middle-aged men. Without them, there'd be no comics."

Sarah spluttered. "That's so *backwards!*"

She was so angry that she forgot to hide her cheek. She looked more beautiful — and strong — that way. "Men aren't the only ones with money."

"Don't freak out on me," Geordie said. "I didn't make the comic. I just sell it. And read it," he said, leering.

Sarah ducked her head, making her hair fall over her cheek, and just like that, the fierce, brave Sarah that I loved was gone. She grabbed her comics and left.

I followed her out. I wanted to tell her that she was fabulous. I wanted to tell her that I agreed with what she said. I wanted to tell her that I'd illustrate any comic she wrote. Most of all, I wanted to ask her out. But Sarah was walking hard and fast, and I let her get ahead of me, and then out of sight, the words still curled on my tongue.

I push the sheets aside and get up, turn on my desk lamp, and rub my eyes.

I pick up my pencil, look at the roughs I did earlier, and start sketching in the details. Sarah and me, fighting crime. I've gotten better. I can see it in the way the lines flow, in the way the characters look more natural, their expressions stronger, the shadows and light enhancing each other. It's like all my fear and pain drive me, pouring onto the page to grab the reader. But I want it to be Sarah who reads these pages, who sees herself strong and fierce like the comics she wanted to buy.

I know my story line is clumsy and my dialogue awkward, but Sarah can fix those when she gets back. We'll be the perfect team.

I finish up the crosshatching, deepening the shadows around the building that Diamond and I leap from before we fly off into the night. Then I cap my pen and crawl back into bed, my fingers stiff, my body so tired that I fall asleep without trying.

I dream of Sarah.

SARAH

SOMETIMES IT FEELS LIKE I've always been here. This shack, this prison, has become my reality. The same damned things every day, over and over again until I want to scream. I do scream. I have screamed many times. But I try not to, because when I do, I feel myself start to lose it. Like I'm falling through the darkness of my mind to a place I'll never crawl out of.

I know the seasons are passing. I don't need the thermal blanket anymore. Barely need my coat. I can smell mud and the beginnings of grass and leaves.

I talk to Dad and Mom, to Charlene and Nick, as if they're here beside me, and I imagine them answering me back. I make up entire conversations. I have to. And I live and relive my memories.

The first time I "met" Nick outside of school, we were both reaching for a misshelved copy of *Invincible*. Nick got it first, my fingers just brushing the comic.

"Hey!" I said, trying to grab it.

Nick whirled around — and then his face softened. "Here. You can have it," he said, thrusting it into my hands.

"No. Take it." I shoved it back.

"What? Why?" Nick blinked behind his thick glasses.

"I don't take pity gestures."

"Pity?"

"My cheek," I said, gesturing, though he'd have had to be blind to miss it.

"Oh." Nick's face grew red. "No, I— Hey, I don't take pity gestures, either."

"What?"

"You know, feeling sorry for the fat loser guy."

I scowled and shoved the comic at his chest. "Just take it."

"Okay," Nick said slowly, reaching for it. "I've been waiting for this all week. They forgot to put it in my pull file, and I heard it already sold out."

I'd heard that, too. "You won it, fair and square. You really did beat me to it."

"Barely." Nick shook his head.

"I'm Sarah," I said.

"Yeah, I know." Nick looked at me. "We're in the same school."

"Oh." My face burned. I ducked my head to hide behind my hair even more. I didn't look at the other kids a lot, especially not at their faces, not unless I had to. I did my best not to engage them. But now I'd probably made him feel like a loser.

I searched through my memory. "Nick, right?" I said hesitantly.

"Yeah. Nick. Anyway—I wasn't going to give this to you because I felt sorry for you. It's just nice to see a girl in here. It's usually only us fanboys."

Nick was right—it usually was only guys, and I didn't always feel comfortable walking in. But I wasn't going to tell him that. "Okay." I turned to leave.

"Hey, listen—you can borrow this if you want, after I read it. Say—tomorrow? Same time, same place?"

"Thanks," I said, smiling at him for the first time. "I'd like that."

I lean my head back, replaying the memory over and over again.

I wake to Brian leaning over me. I know his breath, his smell. I don't know how he got in without my waking up, but exhaustion makes me slower. Stupid.

He's breathing heavily, excited. He rolls me over, pulls off my coat and shirt, then unhooks my bra and takes that, too. I don't bother to fight him. There's an electronic whirring sound, a high-pitched hum, and then a snick.

"What was that?" I ask sharply, my senses suddenly alert.

"I'm marking our time together. Making sure I'll never forget you."

My skin crawls. I prop myself upright, hear the faint, high-pitched whine again, and then the snick. *He's taking photos of me!*

I slash out with my hands, trying to snatch his camera away from him, but he just laughs. More clicks. More images of me, half nude, captured forever.

I struggle to get up, but he's pulled my jeans partway down, and they tangle my legs. He keeps snapping photos.

Fury explodes inside me. I bare my teeth and grimace, trying to create the worst possible vision of me, photos he won't want to take.

Brian laughs softly. "You can make all the faces you want. I'll treasure each of them, and so will my friends. And your parents will get copies, of course. I'll send them anonymously, but I'll make sure they get them, with your face circled in bright red marker. I'll make sure they suffer. Unless you start learning faster."

A sob catches in my throat. I know what he wants. "I was selfish. I made everyone around me suffer," I say dully.

Brian climbs on top of me. "Yes! That's right. And?"

"I manipulated people. Acted like a victim. Especially with my parents."

"Especially with your mom," Brian says softly, his lips close to my ear. He grabs my breast, and I disappear.

SARAH

MANY DAYS HAVE PASSED, but I can't stop thinking about Brian taking photos of me. I keep hearing him tell me that he'll share them with his friends. It makes me feel dirty to know that strangers' eyes will rake my body and get turned on. Makes me feel helpless, like the victim Brian says I am. I can't stop wondering if he's put the photos of me up on some porn site, or shared them with other perverts. God, I hate him.

I was so ashamed when he said he'd show the photos to my parents. But now I almost wish he would. Maybe they could find some clue about where I am. But I know Brian's too careful. He won't really let them see the photos, or if he does, he'll make sure there's nothing identifiable in them. Nothing that would help them find me. I'm so scared I'll never get out of here.

I wish I hadn't been so afraid to be who I am. Wish I'd shared the things that really mattered to me, like my comic scripts. If only I'd shown them to Dad. To Nick and Charlene, too. They would have seen more of the real me. Now I might never have a chance to show them.

My eyes burn. If only I hadn't been so afraid of people's judgment. If only I hadn't tried so hard to be invisible. I should have been all of me, not just a quarter.

I want to live. How I want to live! But not like this. Not kept in a tiny room like an animal in a cage. I almost want Brian to kill me to get it over with.

I shake myself. No, that's crazy. I need to live.

A car drives up. I stand, trying to keep my breathing even.

The stairs shake, and then Brian opens the door. "Honey, I'm ho-oome!" he calls, then laughs as he walks toward me.

Sick bastard.

Brian grips my shoulders, massaging them. "You're so tense. Relax. It's not good for you."

I don't respond. I hate the way he plays with me. I don't know how much more of this I can take. I almost wish he'd tell me if he's going to kill me. *When* he's going to kill me.

"I have something I want you to watch," Brian says. "Well, hear, anyway. So pay attention. Maybe you can learn from it."

There's the sound of Windows starting up, and some clicks, and then I hear faint voices. I haven't heard a computer in so long, it feels like it's from another life that was just a dream.

Brian turns up the volume.

"Please, no!" a frightened girl's voice begs. "I did everything you asked."

"You need to find freedom. Find release," Brian's tinny voice says. "You've got too much pain, and you haven't learned to let it go. So I'm going to give you freedom. The ultimate freedom."

There's a rustling sound. Metal rasps, like a knife drawn from a sheath. The girl screams.

I shudder, sweat trickling down my back. I want the voices to stop. Want to slap my hands over my ears, but I know if I do, he'll use it against me. Probably play it for me again. So I stand still, shaking deep inside, and listen. I try not to wonder how many times he's played this on his laptop.

"Please, I'll do anything!" the girl cries.

"Anything but take responsibility. Oh, you parroted the words back, Judy, but that's not enough," Brian's voice says.

The girl cries out — a high-pitched cry of fear and pain that turns into a gurgle. There's a heavy, wet thump, and then silence, except for the sound of Brian's panting.

There's another click as he turns off the recording.

I retch, trying not to vomit. "What happened to her?"

"You know what happened," Brian says gently. "She found everlasting freedom."

NICK
DAY 98, 6:40 P.M.

I'M HERE SO OFTEN that the Meadowses' house is almost more familiar than my own. I sit with Sarah's mom, and we talk about Sarah. We go on the website together and try to think up new ways to find her. And we avoid talking about the possibility that she might be dead, or if she's not, that she's probably having unspeakable things done to her.

"The psychic said Sarah is still alive," Sarah's mom says, quiet so Mr. Meadows won't hear. "He said she's trapped somewhere and can't get to us."

I duck my head. I don't know if I believe in psychics. I want to. I need to so badly, the way I can see Mrs. Meadows needs to. But if the psychic is just playing on her hopes, taking her money when things are so tight — that would make it even more unbearable. Mr. Meadows gets enraged when he hears about the psychic, I think because he's afraid to believe Sarah's still alive when he so desperately needs her to be. I can see his pain in the new lines in his face, in the deep set of his eyes. But we each deal with Sarah's disappearance in our own way. And Mrs. Meadows's is a psychic. It's easier for me to go there, since I love the paranormal. Love the idea of a superpower.

I squeeze her hand. "That's good news," I say quietly.

"You want another grilled cheese?" Sarah's mom asks, pushing her chair back.

"Sure," I say. "Thank you, Mrs. Meadows."

"Ellen," Sarah's mom says.

But I still can't call her that.

"Grilled cheese — it's one of Sarah's favorites," she says, slapping bread and cheese down onto the frying pan. Her voice chokes off.

"I know," I say. "And she also loves peanut butter and chocolate milk."

"Yes. She does," Mrs. Meadows says quickly.

I shift uncomfortably in my seat. I feel guilty about not having told them the truth, but I needed to be here too much. Needed that connection to Sarah.

But now I have a relationship with them both. A kind of friendship, almost family. I don't know if it's strong enough on their end to survive me telling the truth, but I have to try.

I clear my throat. "I need to tell you something."

Mrs. Meadows freezes, spatula in the air. Mr. Meadows sets down his mug of coffee. Both look at me expectantly.

"I — I love Sarah," I say.

They wait. Nod.

"But I'm not —" My cheeks grow hot. Sweat pops out on my upper lip. "I'm not really her boyfriend. I'm just her wannabe boyfriend."

I stare at their faces. I don't see any anger or coldness or rejection. "We talked, we hung out sometimes, but I was never brave enough to ask her out."

Mrs. Meadows turns back and flips over the grilled cheese. Mr. Meadows takes a sip of his coffee.

"Aren't you going to say anything?" I ask, my voice getting higher. "I'm sorry I didn't tell you before —"

"It's okay, Nick." Mr. Meadows's mouth twitches. "We knew."

"How?" I ask, bewildered.

"Sarah never talked about you," Mr. Meadows says.

It's like he's plunged a sword into my heart.

"Thomas," Mrs. Meadows chides, "look at what you're doing to the poor boy." She turns off the stove, sits down beside me, and pats my hand. "Sarah never talked about you *that* way."

"But she — she talked about me?" I say, my voice a squeak.

"Oh, yes," Mrs. Meadows says. "She talked about your comic art and how talented you are. She said you're going to be famous someday."

I sit up straighter, remembering the time Sarah told me that.

Remembering her belief in me. They weren't just empty words. "When she gets back, I'm going to ask her out."

"Good." Mr. Meadows nods.

Mrs. Meadows gets a sad, faraway look on her face, and her body grows still, like she's not in the room anymore. I want to fix that. I want to bring her back.

"Did I tell you about the time Sarah stood up against a group of bullies, just to protect another girl?"

Mrs. Meadows blinks, then focuses on me. "No, you didn't."

I lean back and tell them — and soon Mrs. Meadows is smiling again.

SARAH

ESCAPE DOESN'T SEEM POSSIBLE, not without sight. I've explored this room so many times, but my hands tell me only so much. They tell me that I'm never going to get out of here.

I'm afraid I'll never have a boyfriend. Never go to college. Never become whatever I was going to become. Nick and I could have been something. A couple. An amazing comic-book team. I wish I'd been less afraid of what everyone thought of me and done more of what *I* wanted to do.

It's not fair. I'm not ready to die. I know life isn't fair; I've known that for a long time. But, still, I want to scream against everything that's happened, everything that got me here.

I don't hope anymore that my parents will find me. It hurts too much. I know they'd find me if they could. And I know, too, that they can't — or they would have already.

The days just keep passing, and the weather, too, is still changing. The foil balls keep multiplying. The ball I made today means that I've been locked up in here for three months. Three months of hell. Ninety-two days of peanut butter, crackers, and bananas. Just the thought of peanut butter makes me gag. But I force myself to swallow another sticky mouthful. I'm not going to die of starvation. I'm not going to die at all if I can help it.

I wipe my fingers along my pants, then take a long mouthful of water, holding it in my mouth to make it last. The jug feels too light. I long to drink more, to ease my thirst, but it's too easy to finish it all, and then have days of thirst far worse than this.

I rub my wrist over my forehead. I am so used to my own body odor and urine stink, I hardly notice it anymore. But I can't get away from the smell of him — his sweat, his sex, his craving me — no matter how hard I try. "My poor baby," I imagine Mom saying, her voice all choked up. I invent things for her and Dad to say all the time.

The lack of human voices really gets to me. I never realized that we need to talk with other people just to know that we exist. That we matter. Loneliness is a howling, empty cavern inside me that just keeps growing.

I shake my head. I almost want Brian to come back just to have someone to talk to. I hate the relief that fills me, the unknotting of my muscles when I hear his voice and know that I won't be alone for a while, that I'll have food and water.

Sometimes he acts so nice to me, almost tender, and I crave that. Then I remember what he's really like, and I hate him — and myself, too. My weakness fills me with disgust.

I want to see my parents so much, it hurts. I want to feel Dad's hand on my shoulder, feel Mom's hair tickle my face as she reaches in for a hug. I want to be reading a comic with Nick, walking down the sidewalk with Charlene, arm in arm, laughing. I wonder if any of them are thinking of me right now. I wonder if they know I'm still alive.

Despair pushes at me, making me heavy. I shove the hopelessness down. I can't allow myself to wallow in it. I've lost whole days doing that.

But it's not like your trying to escape has done anything, a voice whispers inside me. *You're still here, still his prisoner —*

And I'm still alive. That's what I have to focus on. Because I want to live. Even now I can't let myself give up. And that's something I didn't know about myself before — that I have such dogged determination and strength. That I can be completely focused on a goal and work long past what I thought my endurance was, when I have to.

I was focused before — obsessed, really — with the appearance of perfection. But what did that ever bring me but pain? Pain, and not seeing people for who they really are. If I ever get out of here, I'll look at people differently. I'll look for their true selves beneath the mask of their bodies. I'll look at soul.

I take another mouthful of water, then carefully screw the cap back on.

I think I was trying to punish myself by staring at all those perfect faces. Punish myself for how I look, and for the way people treat me. But that's stupid. If I ever get out of here, I'm going to stop comparing my face to others'. Or at least I'm going to try to.

I want to get out of here so badly. I want to walk out the door with my head held high, because they've caught Brian, forced him to tell them where I am, and they've come to save me, the police and everyone I love.

Right. Dream on.

"I am going to get myself out of here," I say. And I know I have to. Because no one is coming. I think, if I'm honest with myself, I've been waiting to be rescued. Oh, I've tried as hard as I know how to escape, tried everything I can think of. But there's always been a part of me waiting for someone to save me — because I *need* them to. But I have to let that go. If I want to get out of here, I have to be the one to save myself.

I stand and walk around the edge of the room — once, twice, three times. The smallness of it presses in on me, sucking up all my air.

"I *will* save myself."

I can almost hear Mom and Dad, Nick and Charlene refusing to let me give up. "You can do anything you set your mind to, Sarah," I hear Dad saying.

Dad would believe in me. I have to believe in myself.

I squeeze my hands into fists. I need a tool to help me escape. Something thin and hard to unscrew the bolts on the door or to use as a lever against the window boards. But there's nothing movable except the food bag, the quilt and survival blanket, the bottle of water, and the smelly buckets of urine and feces.

I touch the food bag again. It's an ordinary sports bag made of vinyl. I feel the zipper pull. Too small, too flimsy to do anything. The peanut butter is in a plastic jar. The drinking glasses are even thinner plastic. There's nothing that can be used as a tool.

Nothing.

I slam the bag down, my hands shaking.

"I can't believe I'm still trapped in this stinking shack!" Even the goddamned buckets are plastic. I heave a bucket away from me, urine and feces slapping the wall and spraying against my face, making me gag. Something clanks against the floor.

I run over and feel for the bucket, snatching it back up, wetness and gook clinging to my hands. I don't know why I didn't notice it before. The bucket has a metal handle beneath the plastic tubing.

I wipe my hands on my jeans, then twist and pull at the metal, my hands slipping. "Come on!" I turn the bucket over on its side, steady it with my foot, grab hold of the plastic handle, and pull. It doesn't move. I yank harder, pull and wiggle and tear at it until the handle detaches at one end with a crack, plastic shards splintering off. Pain pierces my finger, and I rip the sliver of plastic out of my skin.

"Screw you, Brian!" I shout. "I'm going to get myself out of here!" I'm laughing—deep, full-throated laughter. The bucket, the stupid bucket that I hate so much is my key to getting out of here. I can almost taste the fresh air, can almost feel the sun on my skin.

I turn the cracked bucket over and work on the other side. A few more tugs and the handle comes off completely. Warm blood drips down my finger, but I don't care. I am grinning so widely my lips hurt.

I push the metal through the plastic tubing. It feels like it's about half the thickness of one of my fingers, but it's the strongest thing I've got. It will be enough. It has to be.

The window boards are tight against one another, but there's just enough space to get the very tip of the metal in. I push hard, grunting, the metal cutting into my hand. The board groans, then moves slightly. My head is full of laughter. "I'm going home!"

I am so excited that I almost don't register the crunch of wheels on gravel, or the sound of a car door slamming.

SARAH

I WHIRL AWAY FROM the window, the shaft of metal in my hand. The stairs shake. Wood thumps against wood as Brian fumbles with the door. I zip open the vinyl bag and ram the metal beneath the box of crackers.

The door creaks open, fresh air flooding in.

I spin around. I have to distract him, have to keep him from seeing that the handle is gone.

I can hear him standing there, breathing. *Please don't let him see what I've done.*

The floorboards squeal as he walks toward me.

"I hate that bucket!" I scream, my throat raw. "It's disgusting! I need a real fucking toilet, not some smelly, nasty, disgusting bucket!"

He still doesn't say anything. *What is he thinking?*

"I can't take it anymore!" I put a pleading tone into my voice. "Please, can't you bring me something else? Anything else?"

"Shut up," Brian says. "You made a real mess, didn't you? I'll leave you some rags. You can clean it up later."

Silence again. I can't stand not seeing his face, not knowing where he's looking, what he's seen.

"You're filthy, you know that? Absolutely disgusting." He grips my chin and roughly wipes it with a wet cloth, then pulls my face up toward him, and kisses me roughly. "I brought you some food. Not that you deserve it."

Relief gushes through me. "Oh, thank you," I say, my voice hoarse. He hasn't noticed yet. And he's not going to let me die. Not yet, anyway. "And water?" I say hopefully.

I hear the crack of a seal being broken, a cap being pulled off. Water pouring into a cup. He holds it to my lips, and I gulp it down.

Before I am ready, he yanks the glass away. He doesn't offer more, but I won't beg.

"Go ahead. Eat," he says gruffly, putting a long, waxy fruit in my hand.

I can't help it. I tear open the banana and sink my teeth into the soft, sweet pulp. I can feel the prickle of his gaze on my face as I gulp it down, can feel the heat of his body, smell the foulness of his breath. He is taking pleasure in my hunger.

I stop chewing and spit out what's left in my mouth, then drop the rest of the banana to the floor.

He laughs, a short, hard laugh. "You're a real fighter, aren't you? Even after all this time. I like that."

I almost smile at the kind words, the first I've heard in a week. No. I can't let him get to me.

I force my mouth into a frown. I have to remember who he is.

"But you've got to learn," Brian says. "You won't eat the food I bring? Then you won't get any at all."

"Oh, no! *Please,* no — I'll eat the banana."

I crouch down and pat the floor with my hands, trembling. I can't bear to be without food. I've got to play his game. "I'm sorry. I was being manipulative again, trying to cause you pain."

"Yes, you were, weren't you?" Brian says, his voice closer than I thought it'd be.

"I won't do it again! I'm trying so hard to learn what you teach me. I know I was wrong. Please don't take away the food you so generously brought me." The words stick in my throat; I have to cough them out. But I must say them. I don't think my weakened body can take much more starvation.

I raise my head and let him see my desperation and misery.

"You *are* trying to learn; I can see that," Brian says, his hand cupping my cheek. I don't move away. "And I am merciful. I will only take half the food I brought. The rest is a gift."

"Oh, thank you!" I say, trembling with relief. He doesn't

say anything, and I know he's watching me. I stand slowly, the precious banana in my hand.

I wait for his body to crush mine, for the pain to come. *Don't let it happen again, please don't —*

He pushes my hair back from the stain on my cheek, tucks it behind my ear the way Mom always did. "You're doing very well."

His hand leaves my face.

I hear him pick up a bucket, urine slopping from side to side, and dump it out the door, hear him come back and set the empty bucket down with a hollow *thunk*. My face burns.

"I've got something for you," Brian says in that falsely gentle voice of his.

I flinch.

Brian clucks his tongue. "You'll like this. I promise." He grips my arm.

I struggle, even though I know it's no use.

He slams me against the wall. "Hold still."

He lifts my shirt up above my head, then my bra, and I shiver, waiting for him to push me to the floor. Instead, I feel worn cotton rub against my face as he pulls it down. It smells cloyingly sweet and musky, and faintly like copper. He puts my arms through the armholes, then yanks it down over my stomach. It's too tight.

"There. It fits perfectly," he says, delight in his voice. "I knew it would. The two of you were alike in size and temperament."

Choking dread fills me. "Whose T-shirt is this?" I ask hoarsely. "Judy's. It was Judy's," he says.

The girl he killed. I shudder, my skin growing clammy. I'm wearing a dead girl's shirt. A dead girl's shirt that smells like dried blood. The shirt she was probably killed in.

"I almost brought you Heather's, but I knew Judy's would be a better fit."

Two girls. He's killed at least two. My heart clenches tight. I knew he couldn't have kept any of the girls alive, but I hoped I was wrong. I reach down, touch the stiffness where the blood soaked into the fabric and dried, and then I am scrabbling to tear it off me.

Brian clamps my hands together, stopping me. "Now, now. Judy's almost your sister. It's only fitting that you should wear her shirt."

His lips find mine, cutting off my air, and then he is pressing me to the floor.

After he leaves, I curl up in a ball and rock, trying not to think or to feel. Trying not to be. Eventually, I force myself to my knees and pat the floor for my shirt and bra. I search the entire floor, but can't find them. Even my coat is gone.

I shudder, but I don't take off the shirt. Better to wear it than to have him come back and find me half naked.

After a while I force myself to work on the boards again.

SARAH

THE FIRST THING I do each day when I wake is take the metal from the bag, then find the boarded-up window. I keep the bag close by. I count the boards with my fingers, and work on the same one every time, trying to loosen it. I do that on and off all day, my desperation fueling me. I know it's not a good sign that he put a dead girl's shirt on me — a girl he killed. It's like he's getting me ready for the same role. So I work on the board as hard as I can, ignoring the pain in my hands and arms.

My fingers slip down the metal rod and slam into the board. I swear, position the steel again like a lever, and try to force the board to give up its grip. The scent of metal mixes with my pungent body odor. I think I can even smell the scent of dried blood — the dead girl's blood — mixed with my own stink. I wonder how he can want to rape me smelling like this. But he always does.

I ram the metal harder, praying for escape. I'm not sure

I believe in god. How can there be a god when he or she lets something so awful happen? When girls my age get raped and murdered? But I pray anyway, just in case. I yank the rod harder.

The stupid board won't budge. What did he do, screw them in? I want to toss the metal to the floor and give up.

But I don't. If I give up, I really will die here. And soon.

So I keep working on the board, over and over again. If Dad were here, he'd know what to say to keep me going. He always does. Even that day Madison lampooned my face. He got home late from work. I heard his and Mom's voices rumbling, and then he came up to my room and stood in my doorway. I could feel him there, but I just kept hugging my pillow, staring up at the ceiling.

"How're you doing, kiddo?" Dad said after a moment.

I sighed and turned over. "Not so good."

He came in and sat down on the edge of my bed. I leaned my head against his leg, and he stroked my hair. "Kids giving you a rough time again?"

I nodded into my pillow.

"Do you like them, these kids that tease you? I mean, do you like them as people? Do you want to be like them?"

"No!" I said scornfully.

"Then why care what they say? Why even listen to them?"

"Da-aad," I whined.

Dad smiled at me tenderly, but his eyes were sad. "No, Sarah;

I'm asking you a serious question. If you don't like them, then why listen to what they have to say? The people whose opinions you should care about are the people you genuinely like and respect, like your mom and me. And we both look at you and know you're beautiful."

"Da-aad!" I protested again, and tugged my pillow over my face.

Dad lifted it off, his eyes all serious. "I *do* think you're beautiful. And perfect, just the way you are. I don't want you letting anyone else tell you you're not. I don't want you listening to them, okay?"

"Okay," I said.

"Good." Dad leaned down and kissed my forehead. "Now let me tell you a joke I heard today. You'll like this one."

I jam the metal behind the board again and put all my weight into it, my arms trembling. The metal smashes down, my hands hitting the wall. *Holy crap — the board moved!* I feel along the board, shove the metal in close to where it was, and pull. The board creaks and squeals, and one end comes off.

I am crying now, tears soaking the inside of the blindfold. I'm going to get out of here. *I'm going to see you again, Dad and Mom. Nick. Charlene.* Whimpers escape my lips, but I don't care.

I shove the bar beneath the other end of the board and push with all my might. It starts to give.

A car drives up, wheels crunching on gravel. *Shit!* I smack the board back in place, then ram the bar into the bottom of the vinyl bag.

Brian walks in and stands in front of me, not talking. I can feel his gaze on my skin. I try not to fidget. I wish I could see what he sees, wish I knew if the metal is sticking out of the bag or not. If the board is back on right. If there's anything that might make him suspicious.

Every moment I am still alive is a victory. But to be so close to escape and have him discover it would be more than I could bear. I bite my lip until the pain is a knife.

"Tell me what you've learned," he says quietly.

A test. He's testing me. And if I fail — will he kill me?

I can't make my brain work. But I have to. "I've learned . . . that my parents are ashamed of me because of my cheek. That they feel guilty about me and don't really love me. And I tried to act like a victim to get all the attention."

What else? My mind is dark, reflecting nothing back. I try to think, to make my thoughts move. "And that . . . I manipulated people, tried to make them take care of me. I made my parents miserable, made everyone who cares about me miserable. I caused them great pain."

"Very good, Sarah. You learn well. Much better than any other girl," he says. He strokes my cheek with his knuckles. "I'm going to miss you."

My heart races so hard I can hear it thundering in my ears

like hoofbeats. I tense, getting ready to run, to strike out against the knife I know is coming.

But instead he does what he always does. I leave my body as far as I can, returning only after I hear his car drive away. I don't even wait for the pain to stop before I get up and work on the boards again.

NICK
DAY 119, 3:45 P.M.

I KNOCK ON THE DOOR.

Mrs. Meadows answers, her steps slow. "Nick," she says. "Come in." She tries to smile, but we both know what a polite social mask it is. It's getting harder and harder for both of us to believe that Sarah's still alive. But we have to.

I follow Mrs. Meadows into the kitchen and sit down at the table across from her. I don't think she's stepped out of the house since Sarah disappeared, except to be interviewed. Someone has to be at the house in case Sarah calls or finds her way home. At least that's what Mrs. Meadows says. Even though Sarah knows their cell numbers. "She learned the house phone first," Mrs. Meadows said once when I pushed her.

"Do you need me to pick anything up?" I ask.

"No, no, that's okay, Nick," Mrs. Meadows says absently. "Thomas is bringing some groceries home after work."

"You sure?" I know that money's been tight for them. They

had to borrow from friends to keep Mr. Meadows's business going — and even so, they put every cent they can into finding Sarah — ads, more posters, even a private detective. And, of course, the psychic. I can see the strain on them, but they never give in.

"Yes, yes." Mrs. Meadows pats my hand. "I'm fine. I don't need anything. But if you'd like to take some more posters with you when you leave . . ."

"You know I will."

"You're a sweet boy."

"And Sarah's lucky to have parents like you. Parents who love her so much," I say. "Who don't give up."

Mrs. Meadows's fragile smile shatters. She covers her mouth with a shaking hand. "I don't think she thought so. Not of me. She and her dad, they were closer than two people could ever get. But Sarah took everything I said as criticism or as platitudes. And maybe sometimes I did do that. The world can be cruel, and I wanted to help her cope . . ."

Mrs. Meadows's voice trails off, and I wonder if she's just realized what she was doing — talking about Sarah in the past tense.

"She knows," I say hoarsely. "I heard her say to Charlene once" — I screw up my eyes, trying to remember the exact words — "that her cheek made things hard because of the way people treated her, but that it was a heck of a lot better than the deal Charlene had with her dad always cutting her down. Sarah said that at least she had two good parents who loved her."

"She said that?" Mrs. Meadows says, tears rolling down her cheeks.

"Yeah. She did."

"Thank you." Mrs. Meadows takes my hand and squeezes it. "I'm glad she knows."

Present tense. Back to normal. I smile at her, wishing Sarah were here to tell her mom herself.

SARAH

I WORK FEVERISHLY EVERY DAY, every moment that I can. I know my death is near. My murder. I can hear it in the things Brian says, and in the way he talks to me.

I've gotten one more board off, but the remaining boards won't move, no matter how hard I yank on them; it's like they're screwed into the window frame, not nailed like the first two were. The metal bar bends with my weight, and I straighten it out. Some days it seems hopeless — but I'm still alive, and that means I have a chance.

I work at the board again, the metal slipping, gouging my hand. "Damn it!" I throw the metal rod away, and then I am down on my hands and knees, patting the floor and searching for it. When I find it, I clutch it to my chest, sobs bursting out of me.

This would be so much easier if I could just see. I yank at the wretched blindfold. It tightens against my skin, mocking me. I hate it so much.

I yank on the straps again, right at the seam where they join near my ear, the way I've been doing every day — yank and rest, yank and rest — and this time it gives a little. It's the tiniest shift, but it's movement.

I hold my breath and try again, yanking and twisting it as hard as I can, over and over, ignoring the pain pressing into my eyes, my head — and then the seam breaks, the chin strap flapping free. I tear the blindfold up over my head and off my eyes.

SARAH

"I DID IT!"

The constant pressure of the leather against my eyelids, the pain of the strap rubbing against my temples, digging into my throat, is gone. But the blackness is still there. Blackness, and little squiggles of light.

I rub at my eyes, claw at them. *I'm blind!* There's nothing covering them anymore, and still I can't see.

I gulp air. I can't have gone blind. How will I ever get out of here? But I think of Helen Keller, of the way she did things no one thought she could ever do, and I know this won't stop me.

I take a breath and gently massage my eyes. I blink, then blink again, and then I can make out rough shapes. It's like dusk inside. The darkness is grainy, lit only by broken beams of sunlight that stream through the window where the two boards used to be, and through the hole in the door.

I blink harder, trying to keep the panic down. I still can't see clearly, just shapes and shadowy darkness and light.

I swallow hard, but at least I can see that much. It's better than before. It's got to be.

I move to the window, to the boards I know by feel, find the metal bar, and start working on the boards. Shove the bar under and tug, over and over again, until my hands ache and burn and my arms tremble.

I don't know how long I've been at it before I realize—I can see again! I stare at the board.

I was right. The first two boards I got off were mostly fastened by nails. The rest of the boards have screws plunged deep into the wood. But still I'm excited. It'll make such a difference to be able to see what I'm doing.

I move until a sunbeam lights my hands, showing me the grime beneath my long nails, the jagged cuticles, my skin rough and reddened. My fingers bruised. They don't look like my hands anymore. They almost scare me.

I push the bar beneath a board again, then stop. Better to see if there's any other way out, first. I turn to look.

The room is smaller than I thought. The walls are yellowing drywall, not white like I'd imagined, with brown and yellow splotches where I threw the bucket. Water-stained, unfinished planks cover the floor, some beginning to buckle at the edges, dirt caught between their cracks. It's almost more depressing to be able to see my prison, but it's a relief to know the confines. I see the ghostly outline of the bucket I have left, the stench reaching me from there.

I slowly walk around the entire shack. I examine everything — the heavy door, the boarded-up window, the ceiling with a dark water stain like a shadow. I look for weaknesses, for an escape route, but my eyes don't tell me anything that my hands haven't already. Not anything good, anyway. I can see now that the door is so heavy and solid, I would never have been able to break through it.

There's something almost familiar about this place. Something I can't quite figure out. I bite my chapped, sore lip, trying to stir my memories. And then I know. The water stain on the ceiling. The unfinished floorboards, the location of the window. I run my hand down the door frame and stop. It's lower than I remember, but it's there. "Sarah was here" in red Magic Marker.

This is the hunting cabin that became my secret hideout in the summers, near the summer cottage we used to rent. It was secluded, a break from the city, the way Dad liked it. But how did Brian find out? Did Dad tell him?

I bend down and put my eye to the hole where the doorknob should be. The bright light pierces my eyes, and I squint against the pain and wait for my eyes to adjust.

The world is full of color. I'd almost forgotten how many

shades of color there are — the way just one tree can hold so many browns, blacks, grays, and greens in the ridges of its trunk. How leaves can hold so many greens, yellows, browns, and even white.

I try to recognize the patch of trees and sky I'm looking at, but I don't.

I search for signs of people — for houses, telephone poles, electric wires, flags, but there is nothing. Just lots and lots of trees and sky. I know there's a cabin to the right — the cabin we used to stay in. But there must not be anyone renting the place right now. Brian wouldn't risk leaving me here otherwise.

I turn away abruptly.

I can't waste any more time. I can't risk him finding the window like this. I have to get out of here.

I pick up the metal bar. It's a lot thinner than I thought it was, a lot weaker looking, and I'm glad now that I couldn't see it. Maybe I wouldn't have kept trying.

I wedge it behind one of the screwed-in boards, and pull. They're just screws. I can get through them. I *will* get through them. I grit my teeth and pull harder. The metal starts to bend.

I turn it around and tug again — short, hard tugs that shake the wood. But the board doesn't move. I can't believe that all that is keeping me from my freedom are some stupid screws and wood.

A car door slams.

Fuck! I spin around, stash the metal in the bag, and zip it up. Feel for the holes in the window frame, and slap the boards back on. I'm still fumbling with the blindfold, trying to figure out how to fix the broken seam, when Brian comes in.

He strides over, covering the floor fast, his handsome face contorted with anger. He shakes me so hard my teeth clack together. "What do you think you're doing taking the blindfold off? Huh?"

I don't answer. I can't.

He shoves me away from him, his hands clenching and unclenching. "I could kill you."

A scream flutters in the back of my throat, but that might push him over the edge, so I swallow it down. I swallow until I think I'm going to vomit. "You can put it back on if you want to," I say, trying to keep my eyes contrite, not challenging. "I took it off because my eyes hurt."

"Your eyes hurt," he says slowly, disgust curling off his lips. "The blindfold was on you for a reason." He laughs suddenly, harshly. "You were trying to escape, weren't you?" He grips my chin and pulls my face up to look at him. "I told you before. If you manage to escape, I will hunt your parents down and kill them in front of you—slowly, until they beg for mercy. You don't want that, do you?"

I blink at him, unable to speak.

"Do you?" he asks, shaking my head.

"No," I whisper.

He lets my chin go, and I back away.

His face is still nice to look at, but his mask is gone. The cruelty is naked in his eyes and in the set of his mouth. Or maybe it's me who's seeing past the mask of his physical beauty.

I tear my gaze away and stare at his feet, at the polished alligator shoes he's wearing, at the tips of his ironed pinstriped pants. I've got to make him think I'm Miss Compliant. Miss Sponge, who's absorbed everything he taught me. Make him think I'm not worth killing. I lick my rough lips. "I'm sorry," I whisper.

"You know where you are," he says flatly.

"I don't know what you're talking about."

He reaches for my chin again and tilts my head upward. "You do; I can see it in your eyes. You know where you are, and you were trying to escape."

I am trembling, shaking without stopping, jagged shaking that comes from deep within. "I wasn't; I swear I wasn't! I just couldn't stand the blindfold anymore."

Brian lets go of my face, but he doesn't look at me. "I knew you'd try to escape—you're so feisty—but I let you linger anyway. That was my mistake."

"No, no—you can put the blindfold back on. I'm sorry!" I cry.

"Too late." Brian sighs heavily, his eyes filling with tears. "It's time I give you freedom."

Hot liquid rushes up my throat. I swallow convulsively. "I know what freedom is. You taught me."

"Did I?" He looks at me. "What is freedom, Sarah? Tell me."

I can do this. I can regurgitate it back. I press my shaking hands together. *Please, let this be what he wants to hear.* "Freedom is not acting like a victim, not letting people treat me like one. It's not asking my parents to take care of me. It's releasing my family from guilt, from the burden I create."

Brian watches me steadily, and for a moment I'm afraid I've laid it on too thick, but then he smiles a slow, easy smile that lights up his face. "That's right, Sarah. You really have learned what it means. You're the only one who ever has." He rubs at his jaw. "This is all very confusing."

"I know what freedom is," I repeat. "You don't have to show me."

"Oh, but I do. I have to show all my girls." Brian smoothes his thumb against my purpled cheek. "But you know it better than most. So I will delay your release until this evening. Would that please you?"

"Yes!" I gasp.

He nods, then turns away. "See you tonight, then. I really am quite pleased with you."

He walks out, shutting the door quickly, locking me in.

SARAH

WHEELS SPIT GRAVEL AS Brian drives away.

I am so lightheaded, I'm almost dizzy. I can't believe how fast that all happened. Can't believe how easily Brian told me that he's going to kill me tonight.

Nausea rushes through me. I bend over, my stomach heaving, mushy chunks of banana and globs of peanut butter coming up in a sour, smelly mess. I wipe my mouth. For a second I think about killing myself before he can get a chance to — stabbing the metal bar through my own throat. It would be more merciful — easier, somehow, if I was the one to do it.

No. I walk to the bag and feel inside for the piece of metal. *I'm going to get myself out of here.* I start to work on the boards again, my hands already slippery with sweat.

I tear the bottom two boards off, the ones I already worked on. I wish I could squeeze my body flat like a cat and fit through, but there's no way I can. I need at least one more board off, maybe two. Two more boards that are fastened by screws.

I ram the metal between the cracks of the boards and push down hard, the scent of metal strong in my nostrils. The board creaks. I yank out the metal, jam it in the crack a little farther along, and ram it down again. The board doesn't move. I grunt, my arms trembling, before the metal slips from my hands and falls to the floor.

"Goddamnit!"

It's hard to tell what time it is, but it must be at least late morning. How many hours until Brian comes back?

Every few minutes I think I hear his car engine, his feet on the gravel. I work harder, ignoring the pain, just jamming the metal under the wood and wrenching it. The sun starts its descent in the sky. It's past noon, then.

I keep working at the board long after my hands feel bruised and numb. I can feel Dad standing behind me, his strong hands on mine, urging me on. I can feel Mom brushing back my hair, telling me I can do anything. I even feel Nick beside me, laughing softly. "If anyone can do it, Sarah, you can."

I grit my teeth and keep going, working past my sore hands, my weakened body. I force the metal through the gap, pushing and yanking at the plank of wood, back and forth, back and forth, until one end comes off with a loud squeal, wood splintering.

I pry the end of the board from the frame and push it down, away from the window.

More air floods in, soft and welcoming against my face.

Tears slide freely down my cheeks, and I breathe in the air, let it fill my lungs. It smells like leaves and grass and pine.

I look at the weathered board hanging there. It's only wood, after all. Wood and screws. I smile determinedly. *I'm going to get out of here.*

I look at the rest of the boards still on the window, the screws plunged deep, and the smile fades from my lips. It took me so many hours to get off just one board. I'll never do it.

"You will, Sarah," Dad says inside my head. I push myself harder, work as quickly as I can. The next board is loosening faster now, as if it wants to help me escape. Every so often I dig my fingers into the widening gap and put my entire weight into yanking the board. The sun is a deep, vivid orange, closer to the horizon, but not there yet. Sunset is probably a few hours away. I listen with my entire body for the sound of his car. "Faster!" I urge myself, my hands slipping on the metal—and then I get another board off.

SARAH

I CAN FIT THROUGH that space; I'm sure of it. I don't stop to think, just scrabble up onto the windowsill and half jump, half fall through, the earth slamming up to meet me. I gasp for breath, sucking the warm, fresh air into my lungs. The sky above me is deep blue, the sun still lighting up the sky. Tree limbs creak their warning on the wind. I leap to my feet. The summer cabin is to my right, its windows darkened. The cabin Brian must have rented. I can't go there. He could be here any minute.

I whirl around and race toward the trees and the shelter they offer. My breath catches as I run. I look over my shoulder, lose my footing, stumble, and run some more.

I reach the trees, and they pull me into their depths, hiding me, shielding me, maple and oak trees with lush green leaves, and sharp-scented cedar and pine that remind me of him. Branches claw at me, jerk me backward. My legs feel unsteady and weak, like I've been ill for a long time.

Behind me, I hear the crunch of tires on gravel. I run faster. Sobs tear out of my throat. I'm sure I feel a hand on my neck, fingers reaching for my shirt, grabbing and plucking at the fabric.

I stumble over roots and uneven ground, running as fast as I can, my legs heavy, sweat pouring off me. Branches whip my face, drawing blood. All I can hear is my body crashing through the bushes, my heart pounding in my ears. And then my foot catches on a root and I am falling, stones and roots cutting through my jeans.

I stagger to my feet and run again, away from my prison. Away from him.

Please let me escape.

I don't know who I'm praying to; I just know that I am. It feels like I am running in slow motion, every step pushing against gravity. And then I see lights gleaming through the trees, and I stop, my breath torn from me. I'm afraid I'm still lying asleep in the shack, dreaming. Afraid none of this is real.

I whirl around, but there's no one in the shadows. No one reaching for me. I turn back to the lights. There's a house through those trees, and people. Safety?

I stare at the house. Its stone walls, pink and gray and white, look strong and homey at the same time, the rounded windows like friendly eyes.

I edge closer. There's a stack of split logs piled against one side of the house and yellow curtains in the windows. It looks cozy and welcoming. But can I trust it?

I shift from foot to foot. Brian must be on my trail by now; I ran like a frightened horse through the forest. He could be here any minute.

I step out from the safety of the trees, stagger up the porch steps, and bang on the door.

SARAH

"COME ON, COME ON!" I mutter.

A woman's face appears at the door, staring emptily out through the glass. Her graying hair is thin and straight, with bits of pink scalp showing through, and the hazel eyes that are beginning to focus on me look sad. Her face is not a pretty face, not a face that would ever be in a fashion magazine, but it's a kind face, and right now it's the most beautiful face in the world.

The woman's eyes focus on me. "Good god, child, what have you done to your face?"

I cringe before I realize she means the cuts from the branches. "I was kidnapped three months ago. My name is Sarah Meadows." I press my hand against the glass. "Can you let me in? Please? He's coming for me; I know he is. I heard his car pull up as I was running away." I'm babbling, but I don't care. I'm so close to safety, but I don't have it yet.

The woman's hand flutters to her throat. "Kidnapped?" Her forehead crinkles.

"I must have been on the news. You can call the police, my parents, anyone, just please let me in." I am crying again.

"Don't cry, child; of course you can come in." Her hand fumbles at the door handle.

"Tessa? Who is it?" a throaty voice calls, and another face appears — a round, tanned face with squinting eyes and closely cropped white hair. Her stiff violet shirt is open at her neck, revealing a white undershirt, the kind men wear. "Who are you? What do you want?" the woman says through the glass.

"You've got to help me!" I rake my tangled, greasy hair out of my eyes. "I'm Sarah Meadows. I was kidnapped three months ago." My voice cracks. "I heard his car as I was running away. Please, please let me in."

The woman frowns, studying me, her lips narrowed.

I want to wrench open the door and shove past her, but I keep myself still, my body trembling. This might be my last chance. "*Help me!* Please! I don't want to die."

Tessa turns to the frowning woman. "I love you to bits, Eliza, but sometimes you're exasperating. Now move over and let her in."

The woman moves out of my sight, and Tessa opens the door wide.

I rush inside, and she slams the door after me, locking it. I stand there shivering in the shelter of their house. It smells good, like oranges and freshly baked bread. I feel like I've stepped into another world.

"Please call the police!" I twist my hands together. "He said he'd kill me tonight. And he doesn't give up."

Tessa pats my arm. "All right, child; we'll call. Don't you fret."

But they don't move. Eliza's nose wrinkles, and I know she can smell me. I flush hotly.

"Can you call? Now?" I say, my voice strained. I look over my shoulder. One door with a lock won't be enough to keep him out. "He'll be looking for me. I probably made a trail as I ran. All I was thinking about was getting away."

Eliza nods curtly. "If you are who you say you are, we'll know right soon enough." She strides out of the room, then turns around. "You know his name? His description?"

I close my eyes briefly. "Brian Gormley. He works for my dad." I glance back at the locked door. *Don't let him find me. Please don't let him find me.* I turn back around to see Tessa staring at me.

"Dear, is that . . . *blood* . . . on your shirt?" Tessa asks, her eyes stretched wide.

"Yes." I clench and unclench my fists. "It's from the last girl he killed. He put it on me — to get me ready."

"Oh my," Tessa says faintly. "What you've been through . . ."

Eliza's voice sounds from the other room, a deep mutter. I tighten inside.

Tessa pats my hand. "Don't mind Eliza; she's suspicious of everyone. Been hurt one too many times. Now you just come on in and make yourself at home."

She walks ahead of me, and I follow her tentatively, an intruder on their peaceful evening. Soft classical music plays from the radio on a bookshelf. There's a plump green couch and easy chairs, and books on every table. A grandfather clock ticktocks softly in the corner. I should feel safe now, but I don't, not with Brian hunting me down. Me and my parents. God, what if he goes after them first?

Tessa turns to me. "You look fair starved. Guess you could use a good meal in you. You hungry?"

"I should be, but I don't think I can eat. Ma'am, he said he'd kill my parents if I ever escaped. I need to go tell" — I don't know what to call the other woman; they're clearly together — "her that."

Tessa smiles. "Eliza, you mean. My honey. My partner. Whatever word you want to use is fine with me, so long as it's respectful. Go on, you tell her. I'll just cook you up something in case you get hungry."

"No, Miss — Tessa, please, that's very kind of you. But if you could get anything you have that could be used as a weapon instead, I would be grateful. Like knives, or maybe a bat . . . We need to be ready in case he tracks me down before the police get here."

Tessa squeezes my hand. "You poor girl. You're right. My Eliza's got a gun. But I'll go get the kitchen knives, and see what else we can use. We'll protect you, honey, you'll see. Now you go find Eliza and tell her what you have to tell her."

I watch her go, gratefully, and then I run toward Eliza's voice. I find her in the alcove between the living room and the kitchen, an old-fashioned phone sitting on a narrow table against the wall. She hangs up the receiver just as I get there.

Eliza nods at me. "The cops were right glad you turned up safe. They're sending someone over to pick you up. Now, what about your parents? They have to be crazy with worry. You want to phone them?"

"Yes, but can you call the police back first? Tell them Brian said he'd kill my parents if I escaped," I say frantically. "They need to protect them. And Tessa says you have a gun. Please, can you get it? He's not going to let me escape. He killed all the other girls he captured. I'm so sorry, but I might have put you in danger by coming here."

Eliza stands taller, her eyes fierce. "Come on," she says. She walks me to the door.

My heart jumps into my throat. "Please don't turn me out —"

Eliza takes a gun down from the closet near the door, opening the cylinder and spinning it. "What kind of person do you think I am? Of course I'm not putting you back out there. Not without the cops." She takes a box of bullets from the shelf, shakes out a few, and loads them into the cylinder before snapping it shut. "If that man does come around here, well, I'm a damn good shot." She holds the gun in an easy way. "That make you feel any better?"

"Ye-es," I say. I gulp in air. I wish I had a weapon, too.

"We won't let that bastard in; don't you worry. Now come on." She jerks her head. "Let's get the cops on the phone again." She leads me back to the alcove and dials the police. "Yeah, is this the guy I was talking to earlier? Well, Sarah's parents need protection." I stand there while she brusquely tells them why.

Tessa walks in with a wicker basket full of makeshift weapons — knives, screwdrivers, a poker, scissors, a hammer, even a golf club. "Take your pick," she says, holding the basket out to me.

I reach out, my hand hovering over the basket. I've never had a weapon before. I hesitate, then grab a knife. Eliza nods approvingly and hangs up the phone, her gun still in her hand. "You want to call your parents now?"

"Yes. Please."

I stand there, looking down at the phone. It's ancient — clunky and black, a rounded plastic dial with holes at each number, and a bulbous handset attached to the base.

Eliza quirks her mouth upward. "You stick your finger in the hole and pull the dial around for each number."

"Eliza, leave her be," Tessa says. She smiles at me. "We'll just be in the other room."

I want to ask them to stay, but I hear Brian telling me I act like a victim. The words die in my throat.

Tessa and Eliza go down the hall, Eliza talking in a hushed, urgent voice. I stare at the phone. In a few seconds I'll be talking to Mom and Dad. I'll be able to hear them speak to me for real.

I am jittery and out of breath. I don't know what's wrong with me. Yes, I do. I'm afraid everything Brian said is true.

I take a shuddering breath, then another. My parents love me. They *do*.

I set the knife down on the table and reach for the phone, then draw my hand back. I'm not sure I remember what their voices sound like. Will they remember mine?

This is crazy. This could be my last chance to talk to them, to tell them I love them. What am I waiting for? I pick up the receiver — and I can't remember our phone number. I want to scream with frustration as the dial tone bleats at me. I take another shuddering breath, picture Mom and Dad, and the number pops into my head. I dial the numbers as fast as I can, before they disappear.

The line rings once, twice, three times. Why aren't they there by the phone? Has Brian gotten them? But we're hours away, aren't we? I chew my lip, wondering if I should hang up — and then someone picks up.

"Hello?" She is breathless, like she's been running. Her voice brings a flood of memories: Mom holding me as I sob out the pain of Billy teasing me at the playground; Mom standing me in front of a mirror on the first day of sixth grade, telling me that I'm beautiful; Mom standing next to me on the sidewalk last year, politely educating a woman about my face; and always, throughout all the years, her fierceness about making a place for me in this world. A fierceness I used to hate.

"Hello?" she says again, sharper this time. "Who is this? If this is another prank caller, I swear I'll —"

"Mom! Mom, it's me."

There's a silence, then a sharp intake of breath like I've hit her. "Oh my god, I can't believe it! Sarah? Sarah, is that really you?"

There is so much hope in her voice. Hope and excitement and love. My throat tightens. "It's me, Mom. And Mom — I love you. I'm so sorry for everything I said."

"Thomas? Thomas, it's Sarah!" Mom calls. "Yes, Nick, it's really our Sarah."

Nick? I blink. What's Nick doing there? Maybe this really is a dream.

"Oh, honey, are you all right?" Mom is saying. "Where are you? Tell me where you are, and we'll come get you."

She's crying; I can hear it in her voice. I feel myself loved again, treasured. But it's not enough.

"You've got to get out of there, Mom! He said he'd kill you and Dad if I escaped."

SARAH

"OH, BABY," MOM SAYS, her voice breaking. "That's horrifying! But it's okay now. Tell us where you are, and we'll come get you."

She's not listening! "I'm up near the old summer cabin," I say. "Now please get out of there!" I see Brian's face again, hear him telling me he's going to kill my parents, and my heart beats so hard it hurts. I don't know how to make her listen.

"Sarah?" Mom says, her voice panicky, and I know she's afraid I've disappeared again.

"I'm still here. But, Mom—"

There's a click on the line.

"Sarah, is it really you?" Dad asks, his voice hoarse.

Tears fill my eyes. "Yes, Daddy, it's me." I haven't called him that since I was little, but it feels right, somehow.

"Are you all right?" Dad asks. "Tell me—"

"She's all right," Mom says. "She's somewhere near the summer cabin. She escaped."

"The cabin?" Dad says, sounding confused. "Why—?"

"It doesn't matter!" I pound my fist against my thigh. "You have to get out of there. He's going to come after you!"

"Oh, Sarah, honey," Dad says. "I know you're scared. But are you really okay? Did he do anything to you?"

How can I tell him? "He—" I feel Brian's hands on my body, hear his voice grating in my ear, smell his cologne.

"He did, didn't he?" Dad says, his voice shaking. "I'll kill the man who did this to you. Just kill him!"

I have to tell him it's Brian. But I know him. He's going to feel responsible and guilty. The words lodge in my throat.

"Honey, there's someone at the door. Hang on a minute," Mom says. "Nick, would you get that?"

"What? Don't let him answer it!" I shout.

"Sweetie, it's all right. It's probably just Nick's father wanting him home."

I grip the phone harder. "Don't go!"

"She's still here, honey. And so am I. We love you, Sarah." Dad makes a choked sound. "I can't believe it's really you. We never gave up looking for you. Never gave up hoping you were alive. I want you to know that."

Tears burn my eyes. "I know." But I didn't. Not always. Hearing his voice now, I wonder how I ever could have doubted him.

"I can't wait until we see you," Dad says. "Until I can hug you again. We missed you every second of every day."

Mom's voice sounds muffled in the background; she must have covered the receiver. I grit my teeth so hard they squeak.

"Dad, who's Mom talking to?" I ask, fear gripping me. "It isn't Brian, is it?"

"No," Dad says. "It's —"

"Sarah," Mom says, her voice clear again. "There's a police officer at the door. He's come to escort us. We're driving up to meet you."

Thank god. My lungs expand.

"We're coming to get you," Dad says. I hear the jingle of his car keys.

"Do you need anything? Should we bring you anything?" Mom says.

"No. Just come." I want to crawl down the phone line and jump into their arms. I want to be with them *now*, not just hear their voices.

"We'll be there as soon as we can. It's a three-hour drive, but the police escort should make it shorter," Dad says.

"We can take you with us on our cell," Mom says.

I want to stay on the phone with them, as if that'll keep me safe, but I know it won't, and I can't. I've already spent too long being distracted. I have to be ready, in case Brian finds me. I clench the knife tighter. "No — I've got to deal with some things. Just get here, okay?"

"We're on our way right now," Dad says. "Hang on, sweetie. We'll be there before you know it."

I hear Nick's voice in the background, asking something. He really is there!

"Now, honey, I know you want to see her," Mom is saying.

"No! Let him come!" I say.

"Are you sure?" Dad asks, his voice strained.

All those months, Mom and Dad were all I thought about. I longed to be with them — but I'm almost afraid to be alone with them now. Afraid they'll see how different I am and be disappointed. "Yes. Please. I want to see you all." I try to explain so they will understand. "I want to have some of my life back."

"Okay, then."

"We love you so much," Mom says.

"I love you, too." I hang up fast, my hand shaking.

I know they love me. I could hear it in their voices. And yet I'm still afraid.

Damn Brian. Why can't this be over?

I hear the floor creak behind me. I grab the knife and whirl around.

Eliza's standing there, a cigarette in her hand, her gun in the other. "Whoa, girl. Didn't mean to scare you. Your parents on their way?"

"Yes," I croak.

"Good," Eliza says, her voice almost kind. "Why don't you come on into the kitchen with us? Tessa's cooking you up something. And don't you worry — we're ready if that bastard comes by. Windows are locked, shades drawn, our weapons are at hand. We won't let him get you."

My lips tremble. I don't understand why. I never used to cry when people were nice to me. I nod, unable to speak.

Eliza squints at me. "Come on, now." She turns on her heel and walks away.

NICK
DAY 122, 6:00 P.M.

SARAH'S OKAY. SARAH'S OKAY! It's like a song in my head. The air in the car feels charged with excitement.

I can't quite believe it. And I can't believe the Meadowses let me tag along. But Sarah asked them to.

I know she probably just wants me there as a buffer between her and her parents. Or maybe between her and everything she's been through. It's got to be weird to lose four months of your life. But she asked for me. Whatever the reason, I'm glad.

Mr. Meadows follows the squad car clearing a way for us through the traffic, its lights flashing. He leans forward as he drives, muttering, "Come on, come on!" like it'll make us go faster.

Mrs. Meadows twists around to look at me, her eyes stretched wide with shock. "Isn't it incredible that Sarah escaped?"

"It's amazing," I say, and nod. We've already said the same thing six times to one another, but it never gets less amazing.

Mrs. Meadows laughs. "I knew she had it in her!"

So did I. My Sarah is a fighter.

SARAH
6:01 P.M.

TESSA'S BUSY AT THE stove, flipping pancakes. Eliza sets her gun on the table next to her and sits. It looks so Norman Rockwell — the old pine table and chairs, the napkins and place mats laid out at each place, the salt and pepper shakers, and a basket of sliced homemade bread in the center. A clock above the stove ticks quietly. It's stuff I never would have noticed before, but now all this normality seems like luxury. *If* you don't count the gun, and all the knives and scissors laid out next to Tessa.

The smells are so rich — fried potatoes, pancakes, salty bacon, sweet chocolate, yeasty bread. I breathe in deeply. If I could eat the scents, I would be full right now.

"Sit yourself down," Eliza says, motioning to the chair opposite her. She lights a cigarette.

Tessa turns and smiles. "Hey there. Come join us."

I pull out a chair and sit down awkwardly, the knife still in my hand. It feels strange not crouching on the floor. Not being treated like an animal.

I rub my hand against the scarred tabletop. I don't know what to say or do. I feel so out of place in this room, with its yellow curtains like rectangles of light, and the kettle steaming on top of the stove. I can't stop seeing all the shadows, the places someone could hide.

I feel like I'm holding my breath, waiting for Brian to burst through the door and drag me back. Waiting for him to kill me. To kill us all.

I stare down at my hands to calm myself. My skin is roughened, and my nails are jagged and dirty. I don't fit in here, not in their homey kitchen, their clean-smelling home. No wonder Eliza didn't want to let me in.

"I'd better wash my hands," I say, scraping my chair back.

Eliza shakes her head. "I wouldn't. I know it must be hard, but it's best to let the cops see what this guy did to you. Best not to change anything at all. You might be glad later on down the road, when they catch him."

If they catch him. "But . . . I smell."

"Hell, girl—I don't mind that. What I mind is what that man did to you. I wish we'd known and been able to help."

"You're helping me now," I say. My stomach growls. "I'm grateful you let me into your house like this."

Eliza's cheeks grow pink. She stubs out her cigarette in an

ashtray, grinding it down. "I'm real sorry about before. We're just so used to folks playing tricks on us. People around here don't like gays much."

"I'm sorry." I don't know what else to say. "You seem like good people to me."

Eliza nods. "You got that right."

"Now, Eliza, don't you put our troubles on this girl," Tessa says. She sets a big plate of pancakes, scrambled eggs, bacon, and home fries in front of me, and a mug of hot chocolate. "I know you said you weren't sure you could eat anything, but it would please me if you'd try. Food can help a body feel better."

"Thank you." My plate shimmers through my tears, but thankfully Eliza doesn't seem to notice.

"Well, what are you waiting for? Dig in!"

I set the carving knife down. I can't believe how much food Tessa managed to pile in front of me. I cut a piece of pancake, the knife screeching against the plate, and stuff it into my mouth. It's fluffy yet crisp, buttery and light. I've never tasted pancakes this good. My stomach clenches with the need to fill it.

Eliza pushes the glass bottle of syrup toward me, and I pour some on. It's real maple syrup — dark and sweet. I take another bite of pancake, letting the taste fill my mouth before I swallow. I cram in mouthful after mouthful, stuffing in the good feeling.

I forget everything except how good it tastes. I just keep gulping it down. They sit there watching me, Tessa smiling, chatting now and then about the weather, the food, Eliza watching me silently over her mug of coffee. I stuff myself past where my stomach feels stretched, past even where it hurts. I can't seem to stop. It's like I'm afraid there'll never be food this good again.

Finally, I push my plate away and lean back, my belly distended. I feel queasy.

"Well, you certainly were hungry." Tessa grins like I've made her happy.

I can't believe I guzzled my food like a pig gulping slop. I pat my lips with my napkin. "It was amazing. Thank you." But I don't want to think about food right now. I can't.

"You're very welcome, hon," Tessa says, squeezing my hand.

My stomach cramps hard. I breathe through the pain, willing it to go away. I hope I won't have to rush to the bathroom.

A fist thuds against the door — *bam-bam-bam!* — the sound reverberating through the little house.

SARAH

I SNATCH UP THE carving knife, my stomach clenching harder.

Eliza grabs her gun. "Probably just the police."

"Hello?" a man calls, thumping on the door again. "Anyone home?"

"It's Brian!" I hiss.

"It is, is it?" Eliza says grimly, standing, her gun like an extension of her arm. "Well, we'll just have to see about that."

I leap up. "Don't let him in!"

"Of course not, girl," Eliza says. "Tessa, you call the cops again. Let them know he's here. Shut off the lights as you go." She looks at me. "You go with Tessa, and stay out of sight." Eliza stalks to the front door, flipping off the lights on her way.

"Hello?" Brian yells again. "Are you there? I've lost my daughter. Have you seen her?"

I shudder.

"Hold your horses, man!" Eliza shouts. "We're not all spring chickens."

"Come on," Tessa says, grabbing my arm. I follow her so closely that I step on her heels. She pulls me behind her, then snatches the phone up with a shaking hand and dials.

I peer around Tessa. Eliza's at the door, her gun ready. I can just make out Brian's blurred face through the windowpane.

Eliza aims her gun at him. "Haven't seen no girl. Now be gone — we don't like strangers around here. I've got a thirty-eight pointed right at you, case you get any ideas."

Tessa's whispering urgently into the phone. I clench my knife.

"I'm not looking for trouble!" Brian calls. "Just a little help."

Tessa hangs up the receiver and whispers, "They're still about ten minutes away. There was an assault up at the old McFarland place."

"My daughter's got a vivid imagination!" Brian shouts. "She lies even when she doesn't mean to. I hope she hasn't scared you good people."

"I told you — we haven't seen any girl!" Eliza holds her gun steady in two hands.

"Listen — could you open the door? I feel silly yelling. After all, we're neighbors!"

I look at Tessa, my heart pumping so hard I can barely breathe.

"Don't you worry," she whispers, and squeezes my arm.

"I told you twice already," Eliza calls. "You deaf? No girl here. You'd best be looking someplace else."

There's silence. Brian doesn't move from the door.

He knows I'm here. I don't know how he knows, but he does. I shrink back against the wall, behind Tessa's bulk. I breathe shallowly, straining to hear.

"All right, ma'am," Brian calls. "Sorry to have bothered you. I'll be on my way."

I peer over Tessa's shoulder. Brian's shadowy outline recedes from the door. His footsteps shudder on the stairs and then are gone.

Eliza lowers her gun a fraction.

"Well," Tessa whispers. "That was close."

It was too easy. If Brian knows I'm here, he won't give up. "Tessa—do you have a back door?" I ask urgently.

"Sure," Tessa says. "Out through the kitchen."

There's a thud, and then a splintering sound. The back door smashes open, and Brian bursts inside.

Tessa screams and pulls me behind her. I yank away—I have to know what's going on. Have to do something. I clench my knife, but he's too far away for me to throw it at him.

Eliza whirls around and shoots, the gun bucking in her hands, the sound deafening.

"Ahhh! You crazy bitch!" Brian cries, and staggers, his hand flying to his shoulder. He aims his gun at Eliza, and there's another bang.

Eliza shoots again, her gun jerking, and Brian turns and runs back out.

"This isn't over, Sarah!" Brian screams. "I'll get you when you're not expecting it!"

Eliza strides after him, her gun aimed at the open doorway, and fires off another round.

I run after her, Tessa close behind me.

"I got him," Eliza says. "Got him right in the shoulder. Not sure how long that'll hold him; he's one determined bastard. But at least I got him."

The kitchen door is splintered, hanging crookedly by its top hinges. I start dragging the table over, the dishes rattling, knives and spoons falling off and clanging to the floor.

"Good idea," Tessa says, and grabs the other end.

Eliza hauls the door shut, and we ram the table in front.

"Maybe we should put something heavier on top," Tessa says. "Just to be sure." She hurries to the living room, grabs the metal basket that holds chopped wood, and together we carry it to the table, grunting. Eliza's already cleared the table off, so we heave the basket on top.

Eliza's moving carefully; even in the dark, I can see that. My stomach drops. "Eliza — did he get you?"

Tessa gasps and runs to Eliza.

"It's nothing but a flesh wound." Eliza flicks her hand. "He nicked me, is all."

Tessa shoves back Eliza's sleeve. Dark blood runs down Eliza's arm. I close my eyes. *I did this. I brought this on her.*

"Sarah," Tessa says sharply. "Run down the hall; the bathroom's on the left. Bring the antibiotic ointment, some bandages, and gauze from the cupboard above the sink." She pushes Eliza into a chair. "And you — sit!"

"Tessa, it's nothing," Eliza says. "You know I've had worse. Don't scare the girl."

I run as fast as I can, breath pushing out of me. I snatch the supplies from the cabinet, then race back to the kitchen. Tessa's already cleaned Eliza's arm.

"Thank you," she says quietly. She bandages Eliza up, neat and fast. Eliza rests her head against the wall, her face a grimace of pain, and for a moment I see how old she really is. Then her eyes snap open and she smiles. "Bastard got himself worse than this," she says with satisfaction.

My breath is coming in short pants. "I never should have come here. I'm sorry," I say. "So sorry."

"What're you talking about?" Eliza says. "You were smart to. Didn't we drive him off?"

I glance at Tessa, sure she doesn't feel the same way, but Tessa nods. "We couldn't have lived with ourselves if we didn't help."

My eyes burn. "I don't know how long he'll back off. Brian likes to win."

"Fine. Then we'll be ready for him." Eliza reaches down and picks up her gun. "Now I want you two to get away from the windows. Get back to the alcove and stay down."

"I'm not going anywhere," I say, my teeth chattering. "I'm the one he's after."

"All right, girl," Eliza says. "If that's what you choose. Just be ready."

SARAH
6:28 P.M.

WHEELS CRUNCH OVER GRAVEL. I stiffen.

"Let me go see who it is." Eliza hefts her gun. "You two sit tight."

I follow her to the door. Red and blue lights pulse through the windows.

"The cops," Eliza says. "Your boy won't stick around here now."

I'm not sure about that. Brian is crazy determined.

Footsteps pound on the stairs. Eliza opens the door, and uniformed officers march into the living room, their shoes thumping. Large men with big shoulders and hands, staring at me.

I start to hide my cheek, then stop myself. "He was here. He shot at us — and hit Eliza. They saved me, Eliza and Tessa both," I babble.

"When was this?" a woman officer asks, squinting in the dark at us.

"Not long ago. Maybe a few minutes," Eliza says.

The woman officer turns to the others. "Go call it in, then fan out and look for him. He may not be too far off."

"He shouldn't be. I got him in the shoulder," Eliza says proudly.

"I'm Detective Sato," the woman says. She reaches over and flips on the lights.

"Don't!" I say. He can see us now. Shoot us.

The detective looks at Eliza's gun, and then at Tessa's and my makeshift weapons. "You can put those away," she says. "I think we've outnumbered him."

I put down my knife, my hand shaking.

Detective Sato's eyes grow softer as she looks at me, her short black hair shining in the light. "He'd be crazy to do anything with so many uniforms around, honey." She nods like that should make me feel better.

She studies my dirty face, and then the way Eliza's holding her arm. "Are any of you harmed?"

"Eliza got shot," Tessa says. "And Sarah here needs some looking after. She seems half starved."

"I'm okay," I say quickly. "I'm not the one who was shot."

"I'm just fine," Eliza says. "I've had worse than this."

The detective purses her lips, lifts her radio to her mouth, and calls for an ambulance.

"I tell you, I don't need no ambulance," Eliza protests.

"Me, either," I say.

The detective hooks her thumbs through her belt. "You're both going to get yourselves checked out. A gunshot wound is nothing to take lightly, especially at your age," she says sternly to Eliza. "And you, young lady — you've had months away from home, and who knows what done to you. We need to make sure you're all right."

When I open my mouth again, she holds up her hand. "No arguing, now. I'm in charge."

I look over at Eliza's pissed-off face and start to laugh. And then the laughing turns to sobbing.

Tessa's by my side in an instant, gathering me in a warm hug. "There, there. It's okay now. Everything will be okay."

I want to believe her, but I don't know how. I stuff the sobs back down, shudder a few times, and pull away.

The detective's gaze slides over to Eliza and rests on her bandage, then moves to Tessa's white face. "I know you've had quite a night, but I need to get your statements. I can ride with you all to the hospital." She looks at me. "Your parents will meet us there."

"Thank you," I whisper.

The detective nods brusquely. "The ambulance should be here soon."

"I told you, I don't need —" Eliza says.

"Would you prefer to ride to the hospital in my squad car?"

the detective interrupts. "Because that's what we'll all be doing if you don't get in that ambulance. I'm not having anyone hurt on my watch."

"We'll go in the ambulance," Tessa says quickly. "All three of us."

We stand in silence, Eliza shifting uneasily. My mouth is dry, my heart beating hard.

A siren wails in the distance.

I clear my throat, and the detective's sharp gaze snaps to me. "Brian killed other girls before he tried to kill me," I say. "And he said he'd go after my parents. Can you make sure they're safe? And Tessa and Eliza, too? He won't like that they helped me."

"We've already placed a uniform at your house, and I'll make sure we put one here, too," the detective says. "We are taking this very seriously."

I don't know if that will be enough. Brian's intelligent and sneaky. He worked with my dad for at least six months before he made his move, and none of us suspected him. "He's really smart," I say hesitantly.

"We are, too," Detective Sato says. Her foot taps once, before she catches it. "We'll get him."

An ambulance pulls up outside, lights flashing.

"Let's go," the detective says, holding the door open.

SARAH
9:00 P.M.

THE HOSPITAL SMELLS LIKE disinfectant and stale air, and there's so much noise around me — voices on the loudspeaker, nurses talking, carts rumbling, people crying out. The lights are too bright, but I'm grateful for them after all the months of darkness. I sit on the edge of the hard hospital bed, arms wrapped around my chest, feeling naked in the thin hospital gown the nurse gave me to wear. "I'm Lynda, a SANE nurse," she said when I first arrived. She laughed when I looked at her, puzzled.

"It stands for Sexual Assault Nurse Examiner. I'll be examining you today, doing everything I can to get you comfortable, and I'll stay with you until your parents arrive."

She led me into an exam room and explained what she'd be doing. Then she had me strip. Detective Sato couldn't grab my clothes fast enough, especially once she heard the blood on the shirt was Judy's. She looked almost excited. I know she was just doing her job, but all I could think about was that a girl was dead, and I almost was, too.

I shudder now, feeling the pain. Though Lynda is gentle, I can't bear the speculum — or the swabs that scrape at my insides. I fisted my hands and stared up at the ceiling, trying to ignore the pain.

Lynda draws her breath in sharply.

"What?" I say.

She looks at me over her glasses, her eyes sad. "You have some internal scarring," she says. "But the vagina is incredibly good at healing. It shouldn't be permanent or affect your sexual health."

I look away faster than she does.

She clears her throat. "Looks like you've got a urinary tract infection."

I look at her blankly.

"It hurts to pee."

I nod, shame rushing through me.

"That's common after rape, even just intercourse. Don't worry about it; I'll give you something to clear it up."

The physical exam is almost as bad, with Lynda examining every inch of me, clipping fingernail samples, taking my temperature, my pulse, my heartbeat. But when she is done, she lets me take a shower, where I scrub my body until it is red and sore. Then she leads me to a room where she puts an IV in my arm.

"Please, could I have some clothes?" I beg.

Detective Sato comes to the doorway.

Lynda looks at me. "Just one more interview, and then I'll get you some. Think you can hold on that long?"

I shudder and nod.

Lynda sits with me right through Detective Sato's questioning, asking me to tell her everything I can remember about what Brian did. She tries to be sensitive, but her questions make me feel ill, and I just want it to be over.

Lynda smiles at me. "You want me to see if I can find you some clothes now?"

"Yes! Please."

Lynda pats my hand and says she'll see what she can do. "Are you sure you don't want me to stay with you?"

I shake my head. "I'll feel better if I can just have some clothes."

"All right, then. You stay here, and I'll be back as soon as I can."

I sit at the edge of the bed, feeling sore and bruised, emotionally and physically, and strangely removed from everything. I keep telling myself I'm safe, but I don't feel it yet. Maybe because they still haven't caught Brian.

I wonder where Eliza and Tessa have gone; I haven't seen

them since they wheeled Eliza away, protesting over all the fuss. Tessa shook her head and hugged me fast. "You take care, now. Let us know how you're doing," she said before rushing off after Eliza.

I turn and look out the hospital window. It's dark now, and I see my reflection.

A stranger looks back at me. Long hair that's limp even though I washed it five times; shadows like bruises under my eyes; cracked, peeling lips. Pale, unhealthy skin with raw patches from the blindfold, and the purple-red stain on my cheek brighter than ever. Hollows in my cheeks that didn't used to be there. I look like I've been on street drugs. The only thing that feels familiar and reassuring is my port-wine stain. A croaky laugh escapes my lips.

I turn away from the window. If *I* see a stranger, what will my parents see? I can't wait for them to get here, but at the same time I almost don't want them to come. I'm not the same person I was before Brian took me. What if they don't like who I've become?

And what are they going to do when they find out it was Brian? I wish I'd told them when we talked. Oh, god. What if Brian finds them first?

Wheels rumble along the floor. I pull the thin gown closer around me, wishing it covered more. A cleaner pushes a mop in front of my doorway, his cap pulled down low over his face, his blue uniform hanging baggily, like he's lost a lot of weight. He doesn't look at me, just keeps mopping the floor, missing areas, pushing the bucket on wheels closer.

I tense so tight I shake inside and stare harder. I can't see the man's face, but he's about the same height as Brian.

My throat narrows, my voice drying in my mouth. How did Brian get past hospital security and Detective Sato unseen?

I half rise from the bed and make a strangled noise. The cleaner looks up.

It's not him. This man's face is softer, chubbier, his eyes tired and relaxed.

I sag back onto the bed and hang my head. Of course it isn't Brian. But the fear doesn't leave. I *know* he's coming after me. There's no way he's going to let me go. It's just a matter of when. I have to be ready for him. Have to stay on guard.

Quick footsteps squeak down the hall. I sit up straight, and Lynda bustles in, clothes folded over her arm.

"Here you are, dear," she says, shaking out a pair of sweatpants and an oversize T-shirt. In her hand is a pair of sweat socks and some scuffed sneakers. "They might be a little big for you, but they're all I could put my hands on right now. They're my workout clothes."

"I'll get them back to you," I say, reaching for them.

"Oh, don't worry about it," Lynda says, waving her hand. "I can spare a few old clothes. They'll do you a lot more good than me, anyhow. I haven't had time to exercise in weeks."

My eyes water. "I don't know how to thank you."

"No need. I have a daughter about your age. I'd want to know someone took care of her if she was ever in need."

I hold the clothes tight to my chest. "How do I get into them with the IV?" I say, holding out my arm, the tube stretching up to the metal pole.

Lynda reaches over and unhooks the bag from the pole, handing it to me. "You pass it through the armhole of the shirt." She sits down in the chair next to the bed to wait.

I go into the bathroom and change, imagining the clothes as armor. A layer that Brian hasn't touched.

I stand taller, pushing my hair out of my face, and look at myself in the mirror. I do feel better. Stronger. More normal, even if the clothes hang from me like curtains. I tilt my chin higher and try to smile. My teeth are stained yellow, with darker brown spots on some. God!

"Sarah!" a voice calls down the hall.

Not Brian's. Dad's?

"Sarah!" I hear again. I rush out of the bathroom, the IV bag still in my hand.

Dad and Mom enter my room, Nick a few steps behind. I can't move, can barely see them through my tears. They're here. After so many months, they're finally here. They came to get me. To take me home.

"Dad! Mom!" I run toward them, hot tears curling down my cheeks.

Dad closes the space between us, his strong arms holding me tight. "Oh, Sarah. Sarah!" he says, pressing his mouth against my hair. "You're safe!"

But even with his arms around me, his voice in my ear, I don't feel safe. Not the way I used to.

Lynda starts talking to my parents, the detective quickly joining us.

Nick hangs back awkwardly. I reach for his arm and pull him into a hug. "Thank you for coming," I say. "You didn't have to."

"Of course I came," Nick says, his face growing red. "I'd do anything for you."

"Hey. No acting weird just because I've been gone for a while," I say, lightly punching his arm. "I'm counting on you."

"No acting weird. I promise," Nick says, and grins at me, the way he always does.

I grin back at him. I'm so relieved he's here. Just his presence should keep my mom from sobbing all over me, and Dad from making a big production. I can almost believe things are normal again, seeing him.

I turn back to listen to the detective and the nurse.

"Brian? *My* Brian?" Dad is saying, his face stiff.

"Yeah, Dad. I'm sorry."

"What are you sorry for? It's not your fault," Mom says.

"I'm going to kill him, just *kill* him. When I get my hands on him . . ." Dad says, his voice shaking. "That bastard. Asking me every day whether there's been any news of you, acting so concerned. He's going to regret he ever laid eyes on you. I'll make sure of that."

"Shhh!" Mom says, and pulls me closer.

Detective Sato shakes her head. "You'll leave any justice dispensing up to the police, sir."

Dad rubs my back and doesn't answer. He's hardly let me go since I ran into his arms. He and Mom always have a hand on me, touching my face, my arm, my back, like they're afraid to let me go.

Before, I would have felt smothered, but right now all I want is that contact, that feeling of safety. I know it's an illusion — Brian is still out there, waiting for us — but it still makes me feel better.

"He had us all fooled," Nick says. "He even helped me put up Missing posters all over town."

Dad frowns.

Lynda pats my shoulder. "Mr. and Mrs. Meadows, it's my recommendation that Sarah stay here overnight for observation and that she see a psychiatrist before you take her home. She's been through a major trauma."

Her words punch my gut, taking my breath away. "I want to go home!"

"You heard my girl," my dad says. "Don't worry, honey; we're taking you with us."

Mom looks at the IV bag hanging from my hand. "Is Sarah all right?" she asks tremulously. "What is the IV for?"

"Malnutrition, dehydration," Lynda says. "Make sure you feed her healthy food, give her a daily vitamin, and get her to rest, and she'll be fine. But psychologically, it's better that she have someone to talk to."

I shake my head. "I just want to go home. Please!" I can't keep the desperation out of my voice.

Mom squeezes my hand. "We'll make sure she gets everything she needs, and we'll find her someone to talk to close to where we live. But we'd like to take her home now. She's been away for so long."

Lynda sighs. "I understand. I'll get a doctor to sign the release papers." And she leaves.

Detective Sato looks uncomfortable. "If Sarah remembers anything else, let us know right away."

"For all the good it will do us. The bastard's probably long gone," Dad says. "If you people had done your job in the first place . . ."

I stare up at Dad. He never used to be like this — combative and blaming. Even when he was angry, he found a way to be reasonable. This man is someone I almost don't recognize.

Detective Sato raises her chin like she's going to snap at Dad, but then she softens, watching us all huddled together, unable to let go of one another. "I'm sure the detectives in your area did everything they could to find the suspect."

"You're kidding, right? We contacted them immediately, and they did next to nothing. No, we're better off finding the bastard ourselves."

Detective Sato stiffens. "I realize this is an emotional time. But for your safety, if you should find the suspect or he should contact you —"

"I will protect my family," Dad growls.

And then he'll kill us. I smell Brian's piney odor, feel his fingers digging into my skin, see his face as he leans toward me. Even free, I can't get away from him.

"Don't try to take things into your own hands," Detective Sato says. "That never ends well."

"I won't have to if you all do your job," Dad growls.

The detective flushes. "We've made this a priority from the minute we heard that Sarah had been found. And I know the detectives on your case would have done the same as soon as you contacted them. We don't take abductions lightly."

"That bastard had Sarah for four months. Your lot didn't find her."

Four months? I stare at him. I thought it was only three. The floor moves beneath me.

It must be June, then. School's out. Graduation over. I've missed so much.

The detective is talking again, but I don't hear what she says. Instead, I notice how stiff Dad is beside me, how fast he's breathing. "Dad," I say, tugging his arm.

Dad looks down at me, his jaw clenched.

"It's not their fault."

Dad rubs his jaw and sighs. "You're right." He looks at the detective. "I'm sorry."

She nods brusquely. "We've been in touch with your local precinct. They've assigned an officer to monitor your house in case the suspect shows up there. Officers are out looking for him now. Please contact me or your local precinct if you gain any new information."

"Oh, you can be sure we will," Dad says. "Come on, Sarah; let's get you home."

Home. The word feels like warm pajamas, and for a moment I let myself hope that everything will be okay.

NICK

I WALK WITH SARAH and her parents to their car. They never stop touching her, like they can't believe she's really here. I understand. I feel the same way.

I hardly recognized Sarah when I first saw her. She looked like a starved waif. Long stringy hair, her body too thin, almost fragile, baggy clothes that didn't hide how frail she looked. And the fear in her eyes — it went so deep, past anything I've ever seen. It was so vivid in her face, her jerky motions, her cracked voice. And then she raised her chin defiantly, and I knew her. My Sarah.

I can't believe it was Brian who did this to her. Brian, who kept coming around, pretending to be so concerned. The smarmy bastard. I want to kill him. But most of all, I want to protect Sarah. To make things better for her.

Sarah stiffens, and for a moment I think she's going to jump back out of the car, but then she does up her seat belt and clasps her hands.

I get in beside her and cram my backpack at my feet. Mr. Meadows starts the car, but the engine won't turn over. He curses and tries again, Sarah sitting stiffly beside me, her eyes wide as she watches her dad. The engine purrs.

"We're heading home, Sarah girl!" Mr. Meadows says, smiling at her in the rearview mirror. He pulls out of the parking lot and onto the highway, our escort squad car following. Mrs. Meadows turns around every few seconds to look at us. At Sarah.

Sarah's face is tight and still, her hands clenched in her lap. She looks like she's hardly breathing.

"I'm glad you're back," I say quietly, trying not to startle her.

Sarah licks her lips, looking nervous. "I am, too."

"You're my hero, you know." I probably shouldn't be saying this. It's not a guy thing to do, but it's how I feel. "You've always been strong, but this — you amaze me."

"He's still out there," Sarah says jerkily.

"I know." I rub my hands on my jeans. "I'm not going anywhere, not if you don't want me to. We'll face this together."

"Promise?" Sarah asks, her eyes burning into mine.

"Promise." And I mean it. God, do I mean it.

SARAH
10:10 P.M.

THE CAR SMELLS LIKE pine. When I first got in I thought Brian had been in here, that he was waiting for me. Then I saw the pine air freshener dangling from the rearview mirror and forced myself to relax.

I take a shuddering breath. I have to keep reminding myself that Brian's not here.

It feels surreal, driving home with my parents and Nick, the squad car keeping pace on our left. Our car is full of silence. We're like strangers in a small space, shifting in our seats, glances bouncing off one another, pretending to be absorbed in our own thoughts. Without my parents' constant touch, I feel disconnected, almost adrift. I'm glad Nick's beside me, reminding me this is real. That I'm finally going home.

I stare out the window into the inky darkness punctuated by glowing streetlights. The lights reveal crushed soda cans, fast-food packaging, and scraps of tires littered along the side of the highway like discarded bones. The hiss of our wheels on asphalt is the only sound. Lighted billboards mark our progress—beautiful women selling their bodies as much as they're selling the products, but I don't feel that twisted mixture of envy and hopelessness anymore. The ads are so far away from anything that matters.

I twist around in my seat to look out the back window. There's a car behind us; it's been following us since we got on the highway. I can't see the driver's face, but it could be Brian. I can't shake the feeling that he's waiting, biding his time until he attacks. I turn back around.

Our car jounces hard, jarring my teeth together.

"Sorry about that. I didn't see the pothole," Dad says. He clears his throat. "You warm enough, Sarah, or too hot?"

"I'm fine."

A few minutes later Mom turns around. "Did you get enough to eat? We can stop if you're hungry."

"No, that's okay." They're as nervous as I am.

Dad clears his throat. "I know that before all this happened, we had bad news about your treatments." He looks at me in the rearview mirror. "But I promise we'll find the money somehow."

"I don't want treatments." I can't believe I said that. "I mean, I don't think I do."

Dad flexes and unflexes his fingers. "Well, if you change your mind, we'll find a way. You don't have to decide now."

But I can feel his worry — about me, and about money. Something clicks in my mind. I lean forward. "Daddy — I forgot. Brian said he stole the money so you wouldn't look for me."

"Of course we looked for you!" Dad says. "Nothing would stop us from doing that."

"But if you know who stole it, maybe that can help you get your money back?"

"I don't know, sweetheart," Dad says. "It's worth a try. I'll let the detective know."

"Wouldn't that be incredible?" Mom says in a strained voice. "I stopped hoping they'd find out who did it." She looks at me and smiles sadly. "I stopped hoping for a lot of things."

My stomach tightens. Mom losing hope. I always thought that was impossible. All those months I spent, trying to think positive like her — and she abandoned it herself. I'm glad I didn't know. Thinking I could get out of there is what helped me escape.

I can't stop seeing Brian's face, can't stop feeling his hands on my skin, can't stop hearing him tell me he'll hunt my parents down.

I twist around again. The car is still behind us. I know that's what cars do on the highway — follow each other — but they also change lanes and take exits. This one hasn't, except when we have. My skin ripples. "I think that car is following us."

Mom and Dad exchange a glance. "It's not like there are a lot of places they can go," Dad says. "It's a highway."

"I *know*," I say. "I'm not stupid."

"We don't think you're stupid," Mom says quickly. "You've been through a trauma. Of course you're . . . extra vigilant."

Paranoid, she means.

"It *has* been behind us the whole time," Nick says.

I look at him gratefully. "Will you change lanes for me?" I ask Dad. "Please? If the car doesn't follow us, I'll drop it."

Dad glances at me in the rearview mirror, then at the car behind us. "All right." He signals and moves into the right lane.

I twist around to watch out the back window. The car behind us swerves. For a second I think it is going to change lanes with us, but then it rights itself.

"It didn't follow us," Dad says heartily. "Convinced now?"

No. But I know when to drop it. I peek out the back window again. The car isn't there anymore. It's not to the left of us, and it's not behind us, either. I turn back around.

Dad rubs his neck. "The police are out looking for Brian, honey. They know where he lives and what he looks like. They'll find him."

But will they find him before he kills us? I stare out my window. "He's not going to let me go."

"I know he told you that," Dad says, "but coming after you

now that the police know who he is would be stupid. And I don't think Brian's stupid."

No, he's not. But he's crazed. Driven. And he hates to lose. I look back over my shoulder. I've got to know where that car is.

It's not behind us, not even a few cars back. I look to my right — and there it is, coming up on my side. I jerk back around. The squad car is still on our left, driving at our pace. Have they even noticed?

The nose of the car that was behind us edges up beside me.

My heart beats faster.

Then the car rushes past us, so fast that I don't get a good look. But I'm sure the driver was a man. A man with dark curly hair.

I stare out the window again, feeling sick, but all I can see of the car are its taillights weaving in and out of traffic as it gets farther and farther away from us.

It was Brian. I'm sure of it. But if I tell Dad and Mom, they'll think I'm paranoid. Reacting to the trauma. And maybe I am. But Brian does want to kill me. He wants to kill all of us. I didn't make that up.

"You okay?" Nick asks quietly, beside me.

"Yeah . . ."

"You sure? You seem on edge."

Mom turns around to look at us. "What's wrong?" she asks sharply.

"I thought . . . That car that was following us. I was afraid it was Brian."

Dad slaps the steering wheel. "Brian's not coming after you! Not with his face on the news, the cops looking for him, and your mom and me on alert. You've got to let it rest."

I shrink back in my seat. He doesn't believe me. He didn't even try.

"Thomas, you're scaring her," Mom says softly.

Dad grimaces. "Sorry, sweetheart. But I won't let anything happen to you."

"I don't think you can stop him. I don't think anyone can."

Nick reaches over and squeezes my hand, and I squeeze his back. Our car speeds up, trees and buildings flicking past my window.

"He's not invincible," Dad says. "And it's different this time. We're warned. We've got the police on our side. And I will do anything I have to, to protect you. *Anything.*"

It's not just me I'm worried about. Brian's coming after us. He made that very clear.

If I can't stop him, if I'm going to die tonight anyway, then I'm going to die making a difference.

I lean closer to Nick. "Will you help me fight back against Brian?" I ask in a low voice.

"You know I will. What do you need?"

"Access to the Net, and another mind to bounce things off of."

Nick pulls his laptop out of his backpack, and hands it to me. I knew he'd have it on him. "I've got Wi-Fi through an app on my cell. Geek power! So . . . what're you going to do?" he whispers.

"Tell the world what Brian did."

"Anything you want me to do?"

"Research Brian."

Nick slides his cell out of his pocket, waggling it in front of me. "I'm on it."

I log on to my cloud storage, find a pic I snapped of Brian months ago at Dad's office, then paste it into a draft on my blog. I sit there for a few moments, staring at his photo. Then I take a shuddering breath and write out what he did to me, his obsession with birthmarks, the girls he talked about killing. I write until I can't think of anything else to add, and then I read it over. I hope what I wrote will help catch him. I can't bear Brian doing this to another girl, another family.

My pulse jumps in my throat. I need to find the girls he killed and let their families know they didn't run away. Maybe it'll help them to know that. I would have wanted someone to do that for me, if I'd never come back.

I save my draft, then Google "Judy birthmark missing girl."

Something pops up right away. A Judy Evans was abducted outside her house last year, one state away. She was nine years old and had a port-wine stain on her face, neck, and left arm.

I rub my cheek. She was so young! No wonder her shirt was a tight fit.

I click on another article, nausea rushing up through my stomach. They found Judy's body six months ago. The medical examiner said her throat had been slashed.

It was Brian. It had to be.

I glance at Dad, then Mom. They're talking in low voices, probably about my sanity.

I nudge Nick and pass him the laptop.

"Holy shit," Nick whispers. "You think Brian did this?"

"I'm sure he did. Hey — will you read my post?"

"Sure. And I think you're right." Nick hands me his phone. "Look what I found."

I scroll through the article on Nick's phone. Brian's sister, Samantha, had a hemangioma on her face so bad it disfigured her. She turned up dead in the park outside their apartment building, her throat slit when she was ten years old — and they never found the killer. Brian was fourteen at the time. No father, just a mother who went crazy with grief.

My hands prickle. It wasn't Brian who was taunted for how he looked, who came home crying every day to his mother. It was his sister. All those things he said about my parents, about how guilty they felt, how relieved they'd be once I was gone — that must've been what Brian thought his mother felt. Or what he felt himself.

All that talk about my mother crying must have been what his mother did. In some twisted way, he must have been trying to save his own mother.

"It makes even more sense now," I say. "I can't believe you were able to find this."

Nick passes me back his laptop, his face pale. "What you wrote — it's really powerful."

I search Nick's face, but I don't see any rejection or disgust. Just worry for me . . . and warmth. A warmth that makes me feel lighter, stronger, almost happy for a moment. "Thank you."

I go back to my post and add in all the details about Brian's sister, and everything I guess at. I can't type fast enough.

Nick leans over my shoulder, reading. "Send it to me when you're done, and I'll put it out on the social networks. Maybe we can get it trending."

We work in companionable silence, the car tires thrumming over the highway, bringing us closer to home. I feel a kind of satisfaction, almost peace. I'm not ready to die. But now I have a way to fight back. A way to be heard that I didn't have before. And maybe, just maybe, I can stop Brian with it.

NICK
DAY 122, 11:15 P.M.

I CAN'T BELIEVE WHAT Sarah's been through. It blows my mind that she's telling the world the horrible things she's survived so she can stop this pervert. She's got so much courage and grit. I'm amazed she can still talk, never mind go after him.

But that's Sarah. Strong in her heart and soul.

I saw the fear in her eyes after I'd read her piece, though. Like she thought I'd think less of her. I want to reassure her, but words don't seem enough. So I reach into my backpack and pull out the comic I drew for her, the very first one.

"Here," I say softly.

SARAH
11:16 P.M.

NICK HANDS ME A COMIC. Not a comic from the store, but a hand-drawn comic.

I look at the cover, and I recognize myself — as a superhero. It's my face on the cover, only he's made me look pretty and more assured. Yet my port-wine stain is still there; he didn't erase it. I look closer and see a diamond on my chest. He's drawn me as Diamond!

I turn the pages as I read, smiling at the way Nick and I — the way Heavyweight and Diamond — stop the bad guys. As Diamond, I not only have impenetrable skin, am an expert at martial arts, and protect victims, but I also know when anyone's lying and can pull the truth out of them with my gaze. I love that addition; I wish I'd thought of it myself. Nick, as Heavyweight, stops the bad guys from running away by sitting on them. It's funny, but it's also sweet — and by the time I finish, I am crying.

"You doing okay back there?" Dad asks.

"Yeah, I'm good." I say.

Nick sees me as beautiful, plucky, and strong. I can see it in every drawing, in every line of clumsy, tender dialogue.

Nick hunches his eyebrows. "You don't like it?"

"I *love* it." I don't know how to tell him what a huge gift this is. I felt so powerless with Brian. But Nick sees something different in me. He sees Diamond. "It's perfect. The only thing I want to change is Heavyweight. He should have superhuman strength, incredible courage and persistence, and be able to knock bad guys out with one superpowered punch."

Nick ducks his head, but his eyes look happy.

I touch his arm. "Your drawings are amazing. I think you're going to be one of the big comic-book artists someday."

Nick's face loses all its awkwardness. His mouth curves into a wide smile. "Really?"

"Really."

"You believe in me more than anyone," Nick says. "Even more than my dad. Like you think I'll really make it."

"I *know* you will. I'm going to buy your comics someday! And maybe we'll even do some issues together? Me writing, you drawing . . ."

"Of course!"

I smooth my hand over the comic. "I love that you made me Diamond."

"You already were her," Nick says with such conviction that I almost believe him.

SARAH
1:03 A.M.

WE TURN THE CORNER onto our street. I blink my tired eyes, trying to clear my vision. Nick yawns beside me.

I feel a rush of emotion as we drive down our street — happy and sad, all at once. A part of me never thought I'd see my neighborhood again. It is sour-sweet in my mouth, beneath the metallic fear. Brian knows where we live. He may already be here, watching us. Waiting. But if I focus on that, I think my mind will split apart. So instead I watch the familiar houses as we go by. Nothing's changed since Brian took me.

No, that isn't true. The Mercers' front lawn is now a brick driveway, and the Zevins' house is painted white instead of blue. They're little changes. It's still the street I lived on my whole life — yet somehow I feel like a stranger.

I strain to see our house through the windshield. What I see instead are TV vans. Lots and lots of them.

Dad curses and pulls over to the side of the road, the hazard lights blinking. The squad car pulls up beside us. "We could spend the night at a hotel until this dies down. What do you think, Sarah?"

I chew on my lip. A hotel might be better with Brian after us. But we couldn't stay there forever; eventually we'd have to come back—and he'd be waiting. If we stay here tonight, at least we'll have the police watching our place. And I've waited so long to come home. "I'd rather be home. Anyway, the more we're on the news, the more people will look for Brian."

"Are you sure?" Mom asks.

"Yeah."

Dad pulls back onto the road, slowly passing the TV vans, and eases onto our driveway, the squad car pulling up behind us. Reporters swarm toward us even before we park.

Dad shuts off the engine. None of us moves. The reporters are already yelling questions, cameras on shoulders, lights slicing through the night, making it almost as bright as day in front of our house. But dark shapes move around the edges.

Mom unbuckles her seat belt and twists around to face me. "You don't have to do this."

"I want to," I say, my voice shaking.

The reporters are getting louder. I'm surprised the whole neighborhood hasn't woken up.

"Okay, then," Dad says. "Let's do it." He opens his door, and the noise pounds in.

I step out into the warm night, goose pimples rising on my skin. Dad is immediately at my side. Mom joins us. I don't cover my cheek, don't turn my head from the crowd, just let them all see. Nick stands a few steps away, looking awkward and proud.

"Sarah! Can you tell us what happened?"

"Where were you kept?"

"How does it feel to be home?"

The questions are thrown at me, fast and relentless. The reporters' voices are hyped up, their eyes almost crazed, as they try to get their story. I want to run away. Instead, I raise my head and tell them what Brian did.

The reporters get quiet, trying to catch every word. There's one reporter in the back who is watching me intensely, a baseball cap shielding his face, his broad shoulders stiff with tension. I squint against the lights, trying to see him better. Is it Brian? He wouldn't be that bold, would he?

I blink, and he's gone.

The reporters shift restlessly, arms stretching closer with their microphones and recorders.

"Sarah, how did you escape?"

I hold up my raw, battered fingers. "I worked on the boards over the window with my hands, and then with the metal from a bucket handle. It took a long time, but I did it."

"Sarah! I think I can say for all of us — you're extraordinary!" one reporter calls out.

"Thank you." I clear my throat. "Brian's photo is up on my blog. I hope you'll help the police look for him, before he does this to someone else."

The reporters look friendlier now, all of them more human somehow.

Exhaustion hits me, and my legs wobble.

Dad puts his hand under my arm. "That's all, folks. My girl's had a harrowing few months. We'd like to let her rest."

I expect shouts and grumbling, but the reporters part for us.

Our house looks the same as it always did—a narrow, two-story house with white siding—but it's never looked so beautiful before. Lit up by the reporters' lights, it almost looks like it's bathed in sunlight. The blue curtains are like soft patches of sky, light streaming from every window, welcoming me.

Nick moves closer. "You were wonderful," he says fiercely. "So strong."

I hold his words to me, even as my face heats up.

Dad looks around at the reporters still watching us. "Those're all the quotes and photos you're going to get, folks. Sarah needs to get some rest. So it's time for you all to pack up."

Some reporters mutter, others sigh, but most start walking away, pulling their camera crews with them. I breathe out in relief.

"It's late," Dad says, looking at Nick. "We should get you home."

Nick bobs his head up and down. "Absolutely, Mr. Meadows. I'm just glad I was able to come with you when you brought Sarah home."

"Don't go yet!" I say. "I mean —" I turn to Dad and Mom, trying to keep the desperation out of my voice. "Can't he stay? Just for tonight? He helps me feel more . . . normal."

Dad looks at me a long moment, then nods. "Come on in, Nick," he says. "Why don't you call your dad and ask if you can stay." And he opens our front door.

SARAH
1:10 A.M.

I TRIP OVER THE THRESHOLD. Mom catches my arm, steadying me, and we walk inside together. It smells like home — old books and hyacinths. I breathe in deeply, trying to enjoy the moment, but it's hard to relax with Brian out there somewhere.

Mom steers me toward the kitchen. I hardly recognize it. Posters with my face are stacked on almost every surface, piles of dirty dishes sit in the sink and along the counter, and the trash can is overflowing. Old takeout food containers, piles of unopened mail, and dirty dishes cover the table.

Mom laughs self-consciously. "I had trouble caring about the day-to-day things with you missing. I'll get this cleaned up."

"It's okay," I say. It's not just me who's changed — me and Dad. It's Mom, too. Even Nick seems different, more serious somehow.

There's a sharp rap at the front door.

I jump.

"Reporters already? Didn't they get enough?" Dad frowns.

"Or Brian. It could be Brian," I say. I run to the counter and yank a knife off the rack. Mom watches me with wide eyes. Nick hesitates, then grabs a knife, too. I look at him gratefully.

A knock sounds again.

Dad stalks to the door, his body tight. "Who is it?" he yells, his hand on the knob.

"Officer Ridley, sir."

It's a young male voice, higher than Brian's, reedier. I let out my breath in a rush.

Dad opens the door.

A man with round, pink cheeks, cropped hair, and a crisp uniform steps in. "I've been assigned to protect you," he says, holding out his badge.

"Well, good," Mom says.

The officer's clean-shaven face looks only a few years older than mine, and his short red hair, his pressed uniform, and his shiny black shoes make him look like it's his first day on the job.

Fear shivers through me. The police didn't take me seriously. Or maybe they did, and this is all they could spare. A newbie.

I shake my head. I'm being unfair. I should know better than anyone — you can't tell who a person is just from his looks. Just because he's young and probably inexperienced doesn't mean he isn't good.

The officer's gaze keeps darting to my cheek; he can't keep his eyes away. I look back at him steadily, and he flushes.

"I'll check all the windows and doors, and then I'll make a round of the house every half-hour or so," Officer Ridley says, "but I'll try not to disturb you."

He walks off down the hall, and then we are alone again — my parents, Nick, and me. I am still holding the knife, but I can't let it go.

Maybe I made a mistake suggesting we come back home. Brian is probably watching us right now. My skin feels stretched taut over my body, like every particle of me is waiting for him to make his move.

Nick looks at the knife in his hand and laughs self-consciously, then sets it down. Dad and Mom watch me with shadowed eyes. I place the knife on the table with exaggerated motions. Mom and Dad look relieved.

Mom touches my hair. "You hungry? I could fix you some peanut butter and toast."

My stomach lurches. "Not peanut butter. I can't stand it."

"But you love . . ." Mom's voice trails off. She stands there patiently, not pressing me, but I can feel her wanting to know.

"That's what he fed me for four months. Peanut butter, crackers, and bananas. I don't think I'll ever be able to eat them again."

"Oh, Sarah," Mom says, covering her mouth.

Dad's eyes fill with tears.

Their pain cuts through me, amplifying mine.

"I'd hate peanut butter, too, after that," Nick says quietly. "It'd make me want to puke."

"Exactly," I say gratefully.

"You want anything else, kitten? Anything at all?" Dad asks. "We've got all your favorites."

I shiver. "How'd you know I was coming home today?"

"We didn't. We just kept stocking what you love. Figured you'd want them when you came home."

Brian lied. Of course he lied. They wanted me back. I push down a sob. "Maybe later."

Dad looks disappointed. "Nick?"

Nick shakes his head. "No, thanks, Mr. M."

Mom starts tidying the counter.

Dad sees me staring at the posters and picks up a stack. "I'll put these out for recycling. We don't need them anymore."

With their attention away from me, I lift up the leg of my sweatpants, slip the knife into my sock, flat against my leg, and let the baggy sweatpants back down over top. Nick watches me but doesn't say anything.

He's a good friend. I can't believe he's here, after all the times I ignored him or shut him out.

I've got to make things right with him. Whether anything

happens to me or not, I can't let Nick keep thinking that I don't care. But I'm not sure I can tell him in front of my parents. "I'm going to show Nick my comic collection."

"What?" Dad says, the recycling bin in his hands. "You just got home—"

"Hon," Mom says firmly. "I think Sarah wants a few minutes alone with Nick."

I blink. Dad's always been the one who understood me without my having to say anything.

"Oh." Dad's face grows red, but not as red as Nick's. "Right. Okay."

"You wanna?" I ask Nick.

Nick swallows, his Adam's apple bobbing in his throat. "Sure," he croaks.

"Come on." I jerk my head toward the staircase.

SARAH
1:15 A.M.

I RACE UP THE STAIRS ahead of Nick and skid to a halt in my doorway. My breath punches out of my chest. It feels surreal to be in my room again, surrounded by all my things, as if nothing happened. I feel creeped out by all the airbrushed models' faces staring inanely back at me from my walls. How could I have spent so much time poring over those magazines, making myself miserable?

My room looks neater than when I left it — like someone's tidied up my piles of comics, magazines, and clothes, and there's an indentation on my bed like someone sat there regularly. I turn on my laptop, and my Superman screen saver comes up, reassuringly normal. I wonder if the cops went through my computer trying to find a lead. It feels weird to think that there were probably strangers in my room, going through all my stuff.

Suddenly I can't stand wearing the nurse's T-shirt and baggy sweatpants anymore. "Hang on a minute," I say. I grab clean clothes and duck into the bathroom to change. I still look different, and my clothes are a little loose, but I feel better. Stronger. Like I can face things easier. Amazing what my own clothes can do.

When I walk back in, Nick looks at me appreciatively. I feel embarrassed and good at the same time.

"Charlene's with Gemma," Nick blurts.

"What?" I stare at him.

"*With* with her. They're a couple now."

"Oh." I blink. Wow. I didn't see that one coming. Brian actually told me the truth about that. Worry twists inside me — what if everything he said is true? But I know he used truth to make his lies stronger. "Is she happy?"

"Yeah." Nick nods. "I think so."

"Good. She's been through so much crap; I'm glad she's got someone who loves her." I've got to call her. But right now I've got to deal with Nick.

"Listen," I say awkwardly, "I need to apologize to you."

"No, you don't," Nick says so fast, it almost sounds like one word. His face looks wary, closed up, like he's waiting for me to hurt him.

My heart tightens. I've been inside that expression so many times. "Yes, I do. Just let me, okay?"

Nick nods.

"I used to spend so much time trying not to be on anyone's

radar that I ignored what I wanted and who I liked." I sound lame. "What I'm trying to say is — I *like* you — and I'm sorry I never spent much time with you."

"It's okay," Nick bursts out, his cheeks mottled.

"No, it's not. Listen — I thought about you a lot when I was locked up." My voice shakes like china rattling in an earthquake. "I feel good around you. I want to be . . . better friends. If you'll have me."

"Of course I will." Nick reaches for my hand. "You had to know I have a crush on you."

"You do?" It's incredible that Nick likes me the way I like him.

Nick releases my hand like I burned him. "Don't look so happy."

"No! I am! I just — I never thought anyone would . . ."

"Why?" Nick looks at me incredulously. "You're beautiful, spunky, brave —"

Beautiful? Brave? For hiding myself?

Nick takes my hand again. "You never let anyone tell you how to be. You stand up to bullies, protect other kids, even though you don't want anyone to notice you. You escaped the man who abducted you, for god's sake! Admit it. You're awesome!"

Nick looks so sure of me. Like he believes in me. Really cares about me.

I lean forward and brush my lips against his. They're soft and sweet beneath my own. Nick groans, his chest rising and falling against mine.

I yank away. "I'm sorry, I —"

Nick's gaze burns into mine. "I've been waiting for that for three years. Don't tell me you're sorry."

"I — I'm not."

"C'mere." Nick pulls me close and kisses me softly. It feels so good, the way a kiss should feel. Not like Brian's . . .

Rain spatters against my window like tiny pebbles.

Nick's hands graze my back, but Brian's hands flash over top. I pull away.

Nick's lips are parted, his eyes half closed. "You okay? You want to stop?" he croaks.

I feel guilty; I know how much Nick wants this. I want it, too. But not with Brian in my head. Not with the feel of him on my skin. "I'm sorry."

Nick straightens his shirt. "It's okay. I want it to feel right for you."

"It did!" How can I make him understand?

Thunder crashes outside, like a giant boulder slamming into concrete.

I raise my voice. "It's just . . . I had a flash of Brian, and —"

"God. That bastard." Nick clenches his jaw. "How about if I just hold you?" He opens his arms like a question.

I move into them, my face against his neck. We stand like that while the storm rages outside, our bodies pressed together, as though if we press hard enough, the last four months won't have happened.

Standing here holding Nick, being held by him, is something I never thought I'd have. Yet it's the most normal I've felt since this whole nightmare began.

SARAH
1:25 A.M.

THERE'S A BANG FROM the attic above us.

I rip out of Nick's arms, lift up my jean leg, and yank the knife from my sock. "Dad?" I yell.

"I'm right here, sweetie!"

It's probably just the wind. I edge to my doorway, knife raised, and stand there, listening. Lightning flickers through the dark sky like a jagged tear in the world, bright and deadly.

Nick comes up behind me. "I heard it, too."

Dad appears at the top of the stairs. "You okay?" He cocks his eyebrow at my knife.

"I thought I heard something in the attic. It's probably nothing, but—"

"It's just the storm, sweetheart," Dad says. "But I'll check it out if it makes you feel better."

I try to smile. "Yes. Please. But be careful, Daddy."

"You got it, honey," Dad says, touching my cheek, and he starts up the stairs.

Downstairs, Mom is cleaning the kitchen, clanging pots and pans together, but it's a friendly, comforting noise. I strain my ears, but there's no other sound. I wait, Nick beside me, the knife in my hand. My heart's jittering in my chest like a wind-up toy.

Dad comes back down the stairs. "It's all clear, Sarah. It was just a shutter that got loose. I've fastened it."

"Thanks." I sag, the tension draining from me.

"Well, I'll leave you two be." Dad winks. "Call me if you need anything." And he leaves.

Nick rubs my back, his warm hand relaxing my muscles. "Your dad really loves you."

"Yeah, he does." I shove the knife back into my sock and sit down on my bed.

Nick sits beside me. "I know you've been through hell. It's okay if you need to take your time with us."

"I wasn't trying to get out of kissing you!"

"I know," Nick says, and he sounds like he does.

I lean closer to him and kiss him gently, but I can hardly feel his lips this time. My head and heart aren't in it. I pull away.

"It's okay," Nick says before I can say anything else.

"It's not you. I was having a good time before . . ." Something's nagging at me. Something I noticed without realizing I did.

Something out of place. I slowly walk over to my desk. There's a photo tucked under my homework, just the corner sticking out. I pick it up.

It's me — half naked, blindfolded, lying on the floor, my face twisted in fear and anger. *Oh, shit.* I drop it, and it flutters to my desk.

"What?" Nick asks, rising.

"Brian's been here. In my room." I'm shaking again.

"Are you sure?"

I nod. "I don't know when. It could have been weeks ago . . ." But my skin crawls like a spider is skittering across my back.

And then I realize something else. It's quiet in the house. Too quiet. I don't hear Mom banging pots and pans around anymore.

I yank the knife out of my sock. "Mom?" I call.

No answer. I stand, clenching the knife. Nick's watching me like he's not sure what's going on. I don't blame him.

A floorboard creaks in the hall. "Dad?" No answer. "Dad!" I yell.

"Right here," a voice says.

I stiffen, my heart skipping a beat.

I know that voice. And it's not Dad's.

SARAH
1:27 A.M.

I KNEW HE WOULD COME, yet part of me can't believe he's really here. I don't know what to do, but my hands seem to. I start the video recorder on my laptop and turn it to face the doorway. Then I get a better grip on my knife.

Brian's shadow appears in the doorway. His scent fills the room, taking up all the space in my mind.

I feel like I'm moving in slow motion. I raise my knife.

Brian looms in the entrance, his gaze locking on mine. Torn strips of rag are tied around his shoulder, dark brown and red patches showing where he bled through. He laughs — a short, hard bark. "A knife, Sarah? Really? Do you really think you can win a fight with me?"

No. But that doesn't mean I shouldn't try.

Nick makes a strangled sound.

Brian raises his eyebrows. "Well, well. This is a surprise. Two for one, is it?"

"Oh, shit," Nick whispers. He scrabbles across my bed for my Wonder Woman paperweight and hefts it up as he jumps back across.

Brian points a gun at him, pain crossing his face, the red on his bandage spreading. "I wouldn't if I were you."

Nick shudders to a stop.

I can't let Brian hurt Nick, but he's too far away to stab. "Everyone will know you did this," I say.

Brian laughs. "Of course they will. Because you told them in that oh-so-charming press conference you held." He smiles at me almost tenderly. "Do you remember my promise to you?"

Oh, god. Mom and Dad. I think I'm going to puke. "What did you do to my parents?"

"Just tied them up. They're waiting downstairs. I wouldn't want you to miss their departure."

He didn't mention the officer. I have to hope he's still free.

"But now that your boyfriend is here — and you so obviously care about him — I think we're going to have to do him first."

"No!" I say. I try to think. "You said you wanted to give me freedom. Nick doesn't have anything to do with that. I'm the one you want to release."

"Sarah!" Nick says, gasping.

"How sweet," Brian says. "But you're forgetting what I said I'd do if you left."

Sweat stings my eyes, pricks at my armpits. I glance at Nick, at his wide, fear-stretched eyes, his pale face. "I didn't forget. But Nick isn't family. You can let him go."

"Nice try," Brian says, sounding like he's enjoying this.

I take a step toward Brian. If I can just stab his eyes, or maybe his throat . . .

Brian looks pointedly at the knife I'm holding. "Do you really think you're going to do anything with that?" He strides forward and wrenches the knife out of my hand, then twists me around. He shoves his arm under my throat.

I yank against his grasp. He makes a hissing noise as he pulls me tighter, his arm choking off my air, his chest pressed against my back. My throat burns.

I go slack, willing him to let me breathe. He loosens his grip a little, panting, but I can still feel him behind me.

I shudder. I hate the feel of his body against mine, the scent of his piney cologne tinged with coppery blood.

He lowers his face to mine, his sour breath making me gag. "You know better than to fight me. Besides, a dull knife like that can only maim," he says, like a caress. He tosses my knife away, and it clatters on the floor. "I always keep my knives sharp."

"Don't!" Nick cries, his voice breaking. "Or I'll—"

"Hit me with a paperweight, puff boy?" Brian says. "Don't even try it, or I'll kill her now." He tightens his hold on my neck. "Victims need to be saved. But not the way you think."

I feel him tuck his gun behind him, then pull something else out. He slides one arm down to my shoulders, and then presses a warm, sharp blade against my throat. "You will watch your boyfriend die, and then your parents. But first I'm going to teach you a lesson."

I stomp on his foot and try to twist away.

Brian presses the blade harder against my neck. "Are you trying to make me slip up? I wouldn't want you to pass too soon." He drags the knife along my neck from one ear to the other, pain lighting through me. "Normally I help a girl leave quickly. But you made this personal. You're going to beg me for your release," Brian says huskily.

"I'll never beg you for anything." My voice quakes.

"You will." Brian drags the knife along my neck again, the blade shuddering through my flesh, bright and hot.

I stay very still, my breath shallow.

"Hmm," Brian says. "You're no fun anymore." He shoves me away from him.

I stumble, then right myself, but Brian already has Nick in the same hold he had me in, his knife to Nick's throat. I know if I beg him it will only spur him on. But if I pretend indifference, he'll see right through me.

I've got to keep him talking. Talking, not acting. "You're not saving anyone by doing this — you're just creating more pain.

Do you really think your mom felt better after your sister died? She went so crazy with grief, she couldn't take care of you. They had to lock her up."

Brian presses his knife into the hollow of Nick's neck. "Don't you talk about my mother!"

"Why not?" Sweat trickles down my back. Part of me thinks I should shut up, while another part thinks this is my only chance to save Nick. I have to try. "You didn't help your mom, or any of the families whose girls you killed."

Brian jerks the knife.

Nick winces as blood trickles down his neck. His eyes are scared, but they never leave mine, like he trusts me.

God, I hope I'm doing the right thing.

"I can see I let you linger too long. It will be a pleasure to help you find your freedom, after your friend here." Brian traces his knife over Nick's neck.

I can't stand to see him hurting Nick.

"The police know who you are!" Nick shouts. His face is shiny with sweat.

Brian snorts. "So? They'll never stop me. I'm doing what they want to do but can't."

"Like you did with Judy Evans?" I say.

The knife eases away a fraction from Nick's neck.

"And Heather?" I add.

The knife shakes.

"And your sister, Samantha?"

Brian's whole arm shakes.

I try to remember what I learned in self-defense. My mind is blank. But he's already off balance. I've got to keep him that way. "I know what you do. You kidnap girls with birthmarks on their faces. And then you kill them — all because your mother couldn't handle how your sister looked."

Brian jerks the knife back up. "My mom was a saint! She loved my sister; she loved us both."

"Maybe. I'll bet she loved your sister, but I'll bet she hated how your sister looked, hated the way people treated her child —"

"It hurt her!"

The stairs creak, and I talk louder, hoping he won't notice.

"So you killed your sister, didn't you, to make things easier on your mother? To gain her attention?"

Brian stiffens, and I know I've hit a sore spot.

"Sarah — what are you doing?" Nick hisses.

I ignore him. "You were jealous of Samantha, weren't you? Jealous of the relationship your mother had with her . . . because when there's something wrong with one of her kids, a mother channels all her love and attention into that one kid, doesn't she? Practically smothers her. And you — the first child — were left all alone —"

"All right, all right, I killed her!" Brian screams, the knife bouncing against Nick's throat. "But she was begging for it; I could see it in her eyes. Sami was so unhappy. People stared at her everywhere we went. And Mom forgot how to smile. She forgot about me. All she thought about was Sami's ugly birthmark. So I helped her; I helped them both."

I have a bad taste in my mouth, like I might throw up.

Another creak. I wince. *Hurry, Officer!* I wish my back weren't to the doorway, so I'd know when to make my move.

Brian shakes harder, like he's going to vibrate apart. "But Sami's in a better place now. And that's where you're going—"

"You know she's not," I say. "She's probably watching over you right now, sad at what you're doing." I don't believe what I'm saying. Don't believe in heaven or hell. But if Brian does, I'll use it.

Brian's shaking so hard, he can't hold the knife steady. His breath is coming in puffs, like a scared little kid.

"No," Brian says in a low voice. "You don't understand!" He loosens his hold on Nick's throat. "They needed me. *You* need me. I have to make it right—"

A move from the self-defense class I took comes back in a rush. I leap forward, bringing the bottom of my fist down hard on his collarbone, next to his wound.

Brian shouts and staggers. I hit him again, putting all my fear and desperation into my punch. His knife clatters to the floor, his arm hanging uselessly from his shoulder.

Nick jerks out of Brian's grasp. I pull him away with me, sobbing.

There is a deafening bang. I flinch, crying out, but there is no pain, and then I see Brian stagger, see red bloom on his chest, spreading across his shirt, see him fall to his knees, smell blood and oil and gunpowder.

Officer Ridley bursts into my room. He kicks Brian's knife away, slaps handcuffs on him, then finds Brian's gun and rips it out of his waistband, while Brian cries like a child, protesting his innocence.

I take back every bad thought I ever had about Officer Ridley. Every single one.

SARAH
1:45 A.M.

I SINK ONTO MY desk chair, my legs shaking, and turn away from Brian. I don't want to see him, don't want to listen to him, don't want to smell his blood.

A rush of dizziness hits me so fast, I think I'm going to fall headfirst, right off my chair. I put my head between my knees and breathe.

I should be relieved, even happy, but I don't feel anything. Nothing at all.

And then Nick is beside me, pulling me up, and we are holding each other so tightly, it's like we're one person. I press my face against his neck, breathe in his smell, feel his heart pound against my chest. He's alive. We both are.

"You guys okay?" Officer Ridley asks, straightening up and turning to us.

I nod weakly.

"Good thing I was making my rounds," he says.

Brian lies groaning on the floor. The metallic scent of blood makes me gag.

The officer turns to me. "Your parents are still trussed up. I thought I should make sure you were okay first."

"Thank you," I say faintly. I start toward the door, Nick with me, then turn back. "It's all there on my laptop. Just hit stop on the recorder, then play; you should be able to hear the whole thing, and see some of it. Maybe it'll help you with his case."

Officer Ridley blinks, his mouth opening so wide I can see his fillings. "You are a remarkable girl."

I smile a wobbly smile, then charge down the stairs, Nick close behind. My parents are lying on the kitchen floor, bound and gagged, but their eyes are open, following my every move.

"It's okay, the officer got him," I say as I reach for Dad and start working at the knots on his gag. Nick is already untying Mom.

"Are you all right?" Dad asks as soon as I get his mouth free.

"I'm okay. Just hold still."

"But your neck!"

"It's nothing. They're like paper cuts. Nick's is probably worse."

"Is he all right?"

"We both are."

"I'm so sorry, honey. Brian knocked me out from behind, or I would have —"

"It's all right, Dad," I say.

I'm working on his wrists now. The knots are tight, but the rope is stiff and new, and that makes it easier to untie. I free his wrists, and Dad flexes his hands while I work on his ankles, and then Mom and Nick are standing beside me. We hug and pat one another as if to reassure ourselves we're all here. We are alive and unhurt, except for the hurt inside. And that will pass. We've got each other.

Mom clasps my face in her hands. "I thought something had happened to you. When we heard the shot —"

"I'm all right," I say.

"I'm so sorry I didn't believe you about Brian," Mom says fervently. "That we didn't. We thought it was the trauma talking —"

"It's okay. I might not have believed me, either," I say, trying to smile.

"Where is he?" Dad croaks. "Where is that —"

"He's upstairs," I say. "Officer Ridley shot him."

They stare at me.

"He's alive," Nick says. "Which is more than he deserves —" His voice cracks. "The things he said he was going to do to you — to us all —"

I reach for his hand. "You were brave, you know."

Nick squeezes my fingers. "You were, too."

And somehow, the way he says it, I know that what happened is going to go into one of his comics.

"You are both amazing," Dad says. He gently tugs my hair. "I hope you know that now."

"I do," I say. And I laugh. Because I really do. I escaped death twice and won. I stopped a rapist, a kidnapper, a murderer. I'm not the victim Brian said I am. I never was.

There's a banging on the front door. "Police!"

Mom lets them in, and they tramp up the stairs in their heavy boots, their radios squawking, mud staining the stairs. I watch as they lead Brian out. I know I'm not to blame for what he did. And I know, too, that I am strong inside—stronger than I ever realized.

Officer Ridley approaches us, looking almost hesitant.

"Thank you for protecting my daughter," Dad says, clasping the officer's hand in both of his. "My daughter and her friend."

Officer Ridley tugs at his collar. "I was just doing my duty, sir. But I thought you'd want to know—we found a piece of paper on him about a bank in the Cayman Islands. One of the other officers said it might be tied to your case."

I can see the hope light up in my dad's eyes.

"Thank you," he says again.

The door closes behind the officer, and I feel myself breathe freely for the first time since I escaped.

I hug Dad tight, and he hugs me back. I feel safe again, just like when I was little. Except this time, I feel my own strength as well as Dad's.

My stained cheek is pressed against his shirt. It's been a part of me all these years; maybe it's even helped shape who I am — and I'm okay with that. I like who I am now. I know that I'm a fighter — I don't go down easy. Maybe Diamond and I aren't that different after all.

AUTHOR'S NOTE

Every two minutes someone in the United States is sexually assaulted.[1] Nine out of ten rape victims are female[2] — and those are just the ones we know about, who've reported it. Forty-four percent of those are under the age of eighteen.[3] Studies show that the majority of rapes and sexual abuse are committed by someone the victim knows — incest, date rape — but rape can happen anywhere, and knowing how to defend yourself can make a huge difference in your safety. I hope you'll consider taking a self-defense class in your area. It can help you feel stronger, more confident, and more able to protect yourself.

Stained is a work of fiction, but I drew on some of my own experiences with bullying, abuse, and trauma to write it, just as I did with *Scars* and *Hunted*. Like Sarah, I experienced abduction,

---

1 RAINN (Rape, Abuse, and Incest National Network), based on U.S. Department of Justice, *National Crime Victimization Survey,* 2006–2010. www.rainn.org/get-information/statistics/frequency-of-sexual-assault.

2 RAINN (Rape, Abuse, and Incest National Network), based on U.S. Department of Justice, *2003 National Crime Victimization Survey.* 2003. www.rainn.org/get-information/statistics/sexual-assault-victims.

3 RAINN (Rape, Abuse, and Incest National Network), based on U.S. Bureau of Justice Statistics, *Sex Offenses and Offenders.* 1997. www.rainn.org/get-information/statistics/sexual-assault-victims.

imprisonment, periods of forced starvation, mind control, and having my life threatened—though in a different way. I was also bullied throughout my school years—not because I had a port-wine stain but because I was a scared, shy, abused kid. It made me an easy target for others with their own pain and anger.

Like Sarah, I fought back against my abusers, most especially to help protect other victims, and I tried many times to escape (eventually successfully). I also, like Sarah, fought back internally to keep hold of my own truths, goodness, and sense of what was right and wrong. Those things, and my fighting spirit, my dissociation, my writing and art, the books I read, and, later, good people, all helped me to survive and to heal.

I think we need to hear more good-news stories about survivors who've fought back and escaped. We need the hope and strength they give us. I hope *Stained* will be a kind of good-news story, where readers can see that survivors can fight back and rescue themselves.

—C.R.

For additional information from the author about the book, her own experiences, and resources for learning more about self-defense, cyber bullying, body image, and oppression, go to her website at www.CherylRainfield.com. This site is filled with free articles, teachers' guides, book trailers, short stories, and a variety of useful information. You can also visit her blog at www.CherylRainfield.com/blog.